Galley Copy from Publisher

NOT FOR RESALE

FADE (FADE SERIES #1)

FADE

Book 1 of the FADE Series™

By

Kailin Gow

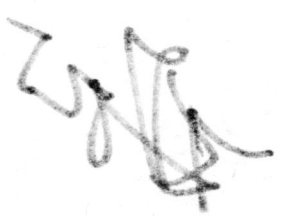

Kailin Gow

Published by The EDGE Books from Sparklesoup Inc.

First Published 2011

Copyright © 2011 by Kailin Gow

All Rights Reserved. No part of this book may be reproduced or transmitted in any form or by any means, graphic, electronic, or mechanical, including photocopying, recording, taping or by any information storage or retrieval system, without the permission in writing from the publisher except in case of brief quotations embodied in critical articles and reviews.

Any electronic copies of FADE that appears on the internet or through sharing in whole, without written permission from the publisher or author, is an illegal copy. Please respect the hard work of the authors and publishers by not supporting illegal pirating activities.

Published by theEDGEbooks.com.

For information, please contact:

Sparklesoup Inc.

14252 Culver Drive, #A732

Irvine, CA 92604

First Edition

Printed in the United States of America

ISBN: 978-1597486163

FADE (FADE SERIES #1)

I mean the flesh, never fade! The flesh never leave the creation, see, because with that divine spirit the flesh cannot fade. If the spirit is weak then the flesh fade, seen?

~ Peter Tosh

Kailin Gow

ONE

My name is Celestra Caine. I am seventeen years old, which makes me a senior at Richmond High. I never thought this would happen to me, but it has... I'm one of those people you see every day, go to school with, remember seeing at the supermarket or the mall, and then one day you don't hear about them any longer. They're gone, and eventually, you forget them.

Not that I'm easy to forget, as much as I might occasionally wish that I were. I'm tall, about five-seven, and I'm willowy. Built for running, my mom always says. Then there's my hair. It's a bright blonde that always attracts attention, from men and women. The women always want to know what I've done with it, and some of them won't believe that it's simply my natural hair color. The men... like I said, sometimes I wish I didn't attract quite so much attention. Sometimes I think it might be better if I blended in a little more.

It's not all bad, though. My boyfriend, Grayson, loves my hair. He loves touching it, and I love it when he's that close to me. I love it when he gives me that look he has that says, not just that he loves me, but that he always will. That I'm the only girl for him. It's worth standing out a little for a look like that from a guy like Grayson.

I first met him running track- he's the captain of the school team, so it's probably appropriate that I'm at practice with him on the day it starts. Then again, I'm at practice with him most days, so maybe it was always going to work out like that. We finish up, and Grayson invites me back to his place for dinner, but I can't. I have to be home, so I tell him that I'll see him tomorrow and get going.

It doesn't take me long to make my way home, since it's not that far from the school. The house is nice enough, in a neighborhood where there's no trouble, and there are plenty of families around. Dad's car is in the drive, so I guess he must have gotten back early from his work as a biochemical engineer. Mom will be there too by now. She teaches kindergarten, and she's

Kailin Gow

always home before me. Even as I walk through the front door, I can picture her in the kitchen, working away at dinner, maybe yelling at my brother, Bailey, not to spend too much time online before he's done his homework. It's just how things are in our house.

Except today, something is different. I know that from the moment I set foot through the door. I can't put my finger on it for a second or two, but then I realize what it is. The house is quiet.

"Mom? Dad? Hello?" I call out, moving through into the living room, then the kitchen. There's no sign of either of them. They aren't there when I check the rest of the rooms on the first floor, either, which is weird. By 6 pm, at least one of them is *always* there.

Still, maybe it's nothing. Maybe the sinking feeling I have in the pit of my stomach is just an overactive imagination playing tricks on me. For all that I still can't help feeling that there's something wrong, it's not like the place has been trashed, or anything. It's not like anything has obviously been stolen, or is out of place. The opposite, if anything. The whole first floor is neat, tidy.

Maybe Mom and Dad have just gone next door for a moment. I latch onto that thought, heading upstairs. Bailey will know. He might not pay much attention to things that don't involve computers, but Mom and Dad will at least have told him where they were going.

"Bailey?" I knock on the door to his room, but there's no answer. Telling myself that he probably has headphones on while he's playing one of those online games of his, I invoke big sister's prerogative and open the door anyway.

Bailey isn't there either. And his room's neat. Too neat. Bailey is, like little brothers everywhere, I guess, a one boy disaster zone. This looks like one of those occasions when Mom has finally gotten tired of telling him to clean his room and done it for him, which means that Bailey couldn't have been back since.

In fact, the whole house has that feel. Like someone has scrubbed it from top to bottom, and no one has been in it to mess it up yet. That probably doesn't sound like a big deal, but for me, it's enough. Enough to send me hurrying around the house, looking

Kailin Gow

for clues as to what might be happening. Because there's *something* happening. I'm sure of it.

I go to search every room again, even though it doesn't make sense. After all, Mom and Dad and Bailey aren't about to leap out from behind the sofa, are they? There's still no sign of them. More than that, beyond the car in the drive, there's still no sign that any of them has even been home.

I check my messages. Maybe there's an explanation there. There's nothing. There's nothing when I check my emails, either. Not even the usual stuff I'd get most days, which only makes me bite my lip harder with worry. I don't like this. I *really* don't like this.

Should I call the cops? That thought springs into my head from nowhere. What would I tell them, though? That something doesn't feel right in my house, and that it looks like a team of cleaners has been through the place? They'd laugh at me, or worse, accuse me of wasting their time.

I haven't called my parents yet, so I try that next. I get out my cellphone and call the number for my father. It doesn't even ring. Instead, I just get this message, saying "Error, number not recognized."

The same thing happens when I call my mother, and when I try to connect to the number for the cellphone Bailey has 'for emergencies'. I've sometimes wondered what kind of emergencies a ten year old can have. I guess now I know. I'm breathing faster now, and I know I'm starting to panic. This kind of thing just doesn't happen in D.C. Not that I know what "This kind of thing" is yet.

I punch in another obvious number. That of my Aunt Chrissie. She's my mother's sister, and my parents always say that if anything serious happens, and they aren't around, I should call her. I'm not sure what good it's meant to do, calling a woman we hardly ever see to come and ride in to save the day, but right now, I'm willing to try anything.

"Error. Number not-"

"Stupid thing!" I throw my phone and it bounces off the sofa, coming to rest on the carpet. I stand there seething with anger at it for a minute, my head spinning as I try to make some sense of all this. There has to be a logical explanation for all of it, right? People don't just... disappear.

Only, I can't think of an explanation that works. Unless I'm willing to believe that my parents and brother have all chosen to visit one of the neighbors together right at the moment when a freak fault has developed in my phone, and what are the chances of that?

This is really starting to weird me out. So much so that I can barely breathe, while my stomach is tight with the apprehension running through it. Nothing good is happening. I'm certain of that now. I just wish I were as certain about what to do next. I need to calm down. To think.

Grayson. I latch onto thoughts of him like a life preserver. He's always been my rock; always been there for me. Whenever I panic about not getting good enough grades to make the track scholarship to Georgetown, he's the one who talks me through it and helps me study. When I'm down about my track times or just annoyed with my little brother, he's the one who picks me up.

Even though this feels so much more serious than that, I snatch up my phone and speed dial his number. For once, I don't get that stupid message, either. Now all I need is for Grayson to pick up.

Come on, Grayson, pick up.

He answers on the fifth ring, though given how fast my pulse is currently racing, it feels far longer.

"Hello?" he asks. "Celestra?"

I'm so happy to hear his voice in that moment that I can't think of anything to say. There's too much of it, and it all sounds so crazy. There's the house, and the emptiness, and the stuff with my phone. For a couple of seconds, all I can do is stand there, listening to him on the other end of the phone like some kind of weird stalker.

"Celes, is that you? Are you all right?"

His use of that pet version of my name snaps me out of it. This is Grayson. I can tell him anything, even the strange stuff. He'll find a way to make all this make sense, or at least a way to make me feel better about it. I open my mouth to explain. To simply say his name.

Before I can get the words out, my cellphone dies. Just dies, without an explanation. There's no power, even though I'm sure I charged it up this morning. It won't turn on, it won't light up, and it certainly won't let me say anything to the one person who might be able to help me. I stand there, just staring at it dumbly, for a second after a second.

The main house phone starts to ring in the kitchen. It's an old thing my dad liked the look of and had rewired, even though we all have individual cellphones. The ring is harsh, cutting through the silence of the house in a way that only emphasizes it.

Has Grayson called me back on the house number, guessing what has happened to my phone? That must be it. I rush through to the kitchen, knowing that I have to talk to someone about this, or I'm going to burst. I snatch up the handset, cutting off that sharp ringing.

"Hello?"

"Celestra Caine?"

A man's voice. It's not Grayson. It's not anyone I know. And yet, whoever he is, he obviously knows me.

Coming here and now, I know the call has to have something to do with whatever is going on.

"Who is this?" I ask.

"Celestra Caine, you are about to fade."

TWO

My eyes flutter open, and I struggle to work out what's going on. Have I passed out? I can't remember. I can't remember anything after the strange phone call. I sit up, and find that I'm on a plush white sofa, in a room that definitely isn't anywhere in my family's house. It's more like one of those chic urban lofts you see on TV sometimes. The ones that look like no one could possibly live there, and they could only ever be for show. The furniture is monochrome, with plenty of glass and steel thrown in, only there aren't any windows, just smooth walls that seem to be made from some kind of metal.

There's a guy there too, sitting in an armchair across from me with a glass coffee table between us. He's maybe three or four years older than me, and he looks like he has just stepped off a GQ cover, with his thick wavy dark hair, square jaw, flawless smooth skin, and elegantly tailored suit that does a lot for his tall athletic frame. Aside from Grayson, he's probably one of the most handsome guys I've met in person. He has one leg crossed over the other, his fingers steepled as he watches me with eyes such a pale blue they're almost like shards of ice.

I sit up so sharply that it's dizzying, and for a moment, I have to lean back against the sofa to steady myself.

"Easy, Celestra."

His accent is British, very carefully refined. Just those words are enough to make me want to know what exactly is going on. I can think of plenty of possibilities-I've seen the news before, after all- and none of them are very nice.

"Where am I?" I ask. "Where are my parents and my brother? Where's my home? And who are you?"

He blinks a couple of times before smiling faintly as though something has just amused him. "I'm afraid you're not in Kansas anymore, Dorothy."

Wizard of Oz references? I'm somewhere, I don't know where, and *that's* the best I get? Well, I'm not some dumb little girl willing to put up with that, and he certainly isn't any kind of wizard.

"Where am I?" I demand, my voice rising. "Where's my family?"

"You still have memories of them?" He says it like it's not that big a surprise, but like it's still something to be regretted. "That's... unfortunate. It would have been better had you forgotten them. They've already forgotten you."

"What?" I can't help that. The word just escapes. "What are you talking about?"

For a moment, the guy does look genuinely regretful. "They faded, just like you, Celestra. Only they didn't keep their memories, the way you did."

I still don't understand. "Are you saying that my parents have..."

"Forgotten you. Yes." He raises a hand to stop me from responding. "Don't worry about them now. They're safe. They're just living a different life together as a family. All three of them."

All three of them, leaving no place for me. I shake my head. "What about me? You can't do this. I'm seventeen, almost eighteen, but I'm still a minor. I should be with them. I shouldn't be... wherever this is. Where *is* this?"

"We're still in the U.S. if that helps," the young man says. "But like I said, you're not in Kansas anymore. You're off the map, down the rabbit hole, and so far through the looking glass that going back... well, that probably won't ever happen, Celestra."

For a moment, I can't help the anger that wells up in me. "How about you stop spouting stupid quotes from literature and tell me something useful? I have rights, you know."

He shrugs. Apparently, my anger doesn't make that much difference to him. "You're in an undisclosed location, and it's better for you to not know where you are right now."

He stands then, moving across to one of the walls, where there's a small kitchen area recessed into it. He opens a drawer, pulling out a tray piled high with fruit and bread and returning to set it down on the glass table.

"You must be hungry."

The food looks good, and my body tells me that I haven't eaten in a while, though exactly how long, I don't know. I won't let myself be distracted by something like that, though. Not when I still don't have any answers.

"I want to know what's going on," I say, folding my arms. "You haven't told me a thing about who you are and what's going on. I mean, you dress like some kind of TV spy or something, but you could be anybody. And as for that crap about my parents forgetting me, I'm not buying that. Where are they?"

The young man sighs then. "Look, Ms. Caine...Celestra, in time you will find out what this is about, but right now everything I say will come as too much of a shock to you, and there isn't time for that. Your parents are safe; your brother is safe. That's really all I can tell you."

"Not even your name?" I demand.

It takes him a moment to answer. Is he making something up, or just deciding whether to tell me?

"Jack Simple."

Making it up then, because that couldn't be someone's real name. "Why not just call yourself John Doe and have done with it?"

He, Jack, doesn't smile. "You need to start eating, Celestra. You'll need all the energy you can get."

My thin thread of fear is back. I still have no idea what is going to happen to me.

"Why?" I ask, and he moves around the table, drawing me to my feet. Moving me a little way from the table too, I notice.

"Because," Jack whispers, and this close, he only *has* to whisper, "you are in a great deal of danger."

At that instant, the wall nearest to us explodes inwards in a shower of dust and debris as something plows into the spot where we were both just sitting. Jack is between me and the worst of it, his suit taking a covering of dust as he pushes me back away from the breach. Away from the military-grade Humvee that has just come straight through it.

FADE (FADE SERIES #1)

There are men clambering out of it, wearing black from their roll neck sweaters down to their combat boots. They're armed, with vicious looking sub-machine guns, but then... Jack has a gun of his own. It's a sleek, efficient looking pistol, which he has raised even before I've finished flinching at the initial crash of the Humvee into the room. He fires three swift shots, and the black-clothed men scramble for cover behind their vehicle.

Jack grabs my arm then, dragging me to one side of the room. The wall seems almost to melt away, revealing a corridor. "Run if you want to live."

I run. I run so fast that Jack can barely keep up with me. Gunfire sounds behind us in a chatter of automatic fire, and Jack turns, firing another couple of shots back down the corridor behind us. We round a corner and he gestures for me to stop.

"Down there."

'There' is an air duct, whose grill swings open as I pull it. While I'm doing that, Jack is busy firing back around the corner.

"You can't be serious," I say.

"Do I look like I'm joking? Now hurry up. It's only a matter of time before they start using grenades."

He's serious. I climb in, and climb down, half crawling, half sliding. This definitely isn't any normal air duct. Real ones aren't big enough to climb through, and they generally have things like fans in the way. This is an escape route. Jack planned for this possibility.

The air duct opens out onto a street, where cool air blows around me, and the sky above is dark. The building I've just come out of is a large one, like an apartment block. For a second, just a second, I think about running, but then Jack is there beside me, clambering out of the duct. He pulls something from an inside pocket, a device that looks to me like a garage door opener, and presses the button.

The building beside us is rocked by an explosion, several windows crashing outward in gouts of flame. Smoke pours from the air duct we've just come down.

"That's just enough to keep them away for a while," Jack says, like it's the most natural thing in the world to have just blown up a building. "Come on."

Thanks to the grip he takes on my upper arm, I don't really have a choice as he leads me to a small lot behind the building, where there's an expensive looking sports car parked. I must admit to liking the look of it. Hey, I'm a runner. I *like* things that go fast.

Jack smiles. He must have noticed me admiring the car. "A beauty, isn't she? An Aston Martin DB9. Certainly the fastest getaway car I have ever had for an assignment. Now hop in, before our friends come after us."

FADE (FADE SERIES #1)

I do it, but I also latch onto the key word there. "Assignment?"

"Fading someone." He puts the car in gear and sets off. I expect him to drive a hundred miles an hour, but actually, he just slips into traffic quietly. "That's making sure they disappear without a trace, like they never existed. Usually, it's for their protection, as in your family's case." I see him glance my way then. "In yours... I'm not so sure. You're a special case, something we've never seen before or encountered. It's a privilege for them to trust me with such an important assignment."

I return his look with interest. I'm not just someone's assignment. Even the assignment of some good looking guy who's so confident of himself. I apparently have armed men chasing me, and I need more than that kind of cockiness right now.

Jack seems to get that, because his expression turns apologetic. "Look, Celestra, I think I know what you're going through...you're scared, you don't know what's going to happen next, you want your old life back." His hand reaches over to pat mine. "And I wish I could make this easier on you, but you can't have your old life back again. You're in a lot of danger, and you're going to need to trust me if you want to get through it."

"Trust you?" I ask. "I don't even know you."

"I know," Jack says, glancing at the road just long enough to overtake the car in front. "But you still have to. This danger isn't just to you. It's to your parents, brother, aunt..."

Everyone I might care about, in other words. Which raises one obvious question. "What about Grayson? He's my-"

"Boyfriend, I know." Jack says it evenly. "I had to watch you for several weeks before all this. I saw you at track practice with him."

"That's very... creepy." Well, what else can I call it when a guy, even some kind of secret agent assigned to protect me, stalks me like that?

"Well, can I say that, as someone who has stalked you, you are a very interesting young woman, Celestra Caine?"

"And that just makes you sound like some kind of pervert," I snap.

Jack seems faintly amused by my anger. I'm glad one of us is.

"But that's not the reason why I had to watch you," he says after a second. "It's because, Celestra, you could pose a danger to everyone."

THREE

The car takes us out onto the highway, and I guess I could get some sense of where I am from just looking at the road signs if I wanted, but I'm too busy trying not to cry. I'm shaking slightly, and I have to blink back tears several times as Jack drives on, only glancing over at me a few times. What will he think, with me like this?

"It's just adrenaline," he says.

"What?"

"The shaking. It's your body coming down from the adrenaline it used in running away."

He says it calmly, like there's nothing out of the ordinary about spending time nearly crying after having been shot at by guys with machine guns, or your family disappearing, or any of the other stuff that has happened to me so far tonight.

"There should be something to eat in the glove compartment," Jack adds. "You'll feel better if you eat."

There are sandwiches there. Turkey and cheese, which is fine, but I still don't bite down on it.

"If you'd rather have something else, I can find somewhere to stop," Jack says.

I shake my head. "It's not the sandwich." I look out of the window for a moment, watching the outside world go past. Like everything else this evening, it's flashing by too fast. "It's everything. I mean, I came home today thinking everything would be... you know, *normal*. Instead, everything's turned upside down, and I still don't know why."

I turn back to Jack then. He's concentrating on the road, but I get the feeling that's at least partly just an excuse. "I saw the goons back at your place. My family's missing, and I can't contact them. Do you want to give me a reason why I shouldn't make you turn this car around and drop me at either my house or Grayson's?"

Though how exactly I would make him do anything, I don't know.

Jack shakes his head. "Your home isn't safe. Nor is Grayson's."

"I can deal with it. I'll take my chances."

He looks at me then. Looks at me with the full depth of those clear blue eyes of his. "Listen, Celes-"

"Don't call me that," I tell him. "Only people I trust get to call me that."

"Then I'm *going* to call you that, because you need to start trusting me if you want to live. Now just listen. You can't go back. Until we manage to fade you completely, we can't even risk you setting foot in your town. I can't let you."

"Let me?" He makes it sound like I'm a kid, not seventeen. He's not *that* much older than me.

"Let you," Jack repeats. "I might not understand my orders sometimes, Celes, but right now, my instructions from the Underground are clear. I'm to guard you with my life. Now, I don't plan on giving up my life just because you want to go home, or because you won't listen." He runs a hand through his hair. "Until this is over, you have to stay put with me."

"And everything will make sense when we get to this Underground?" I can't keep the sarcasm out of my voice. It all sounds a bit too James Bond for me. "You haven't even told me exactly who they are, and what they do."

Jack is watching the road again. "When we get to the Underground, you will be briefed as to what is going on. As for elaborating on what we're part of, it's classified. Sorry."

"Classified?"

Jack shrugs. "We work in secrecy to keep many people safe, and if we breach that secrecy, their lives would be forfeited. Can you understand that?" His tone softens a little then. "I'm sorry, I can't tell you more. It's how we work, and it really would be bad if things went wrong. People would get hurt. People like your family."

Meaning that I don't get to know anything. I sigh, looking round for some sign of where we are. We've left town a fair way behind now, but we could be going almost anywhere.

"How long is it going to take to get there?" I ask. At least that way, I'll have some idea of where it could be.

"If you eat and go to sleep, we'll get there faster. If not, it's going to be a long ride." Jack smiles then. "Not that I'm not enjoying your company, but believe me, traveling hundreds of miles by car isn't exactly fun, even in something that can eat up the miles."

Not the precise answer I was hoping for, but it will have to do. I do eat, getting through the sandwich I'm holding and the one left in the glove compartment with a speed that comes from hunger. They aren't bad at all.

Jack looks over. "You realize those were supposed to last us both the whole trip?"

"Sorry, I thought-"

"That's ok," Jack says, waving it away. "It'll be an excuse for us to get out and stretch our legs at some dive along the way."

I have to smile at that. His accent isn't made for words like 'dive'. He doesn't talk much after that, though, just powering the car on through the night at speeds that have very little to do with the speed limits. He only slows occasionally, usually just in time to avoid going past a cop car at a hundred and twenty.

We've been driving for more than a couple of hours when he points up at a sign. "There we go."

"What?" I jerk to full wakefulness, having fallen into that kind of half-sleep you get on long journeys. "Where?"

"A nice little out of the way stop to eat. I love discovering these places."

He pulls off at the next exit, where there's a tiny diner and gas station. It doesn't look like much as we park. In fact, it looks like the kind of place that is only a week or two from closing down. Jack gets out of the car and goes around to the trunk, taking out a duffle bag before we head in.

The diner is practically empty. There are three guys over in the corner, dressed like truckers, but other than that, it's dead. A waitress who is obviously used to the quiet hurries over and shows us to a table, then says that she'll get menus.

"Which way are the restrooms?" I ask, before she can go.

"Just through the back beside the counter, honey."

I stand, and Jack puts a hand on my arm. "What?" I demand. "Does the whole never leaving my side routine extend to this too?"

Jack shakes his head, and holds out the duffle bag. "I just thought you might want this."

I take it with me, discovering once I'm in there that it contains toiletries as well as a change of clothes. There are jeans and a nice chiffon blouse that is nicer than most of the stuff I wear at home. That's a little surprising. Guys that young don't normally know how to pack for women.

I clean up a little and change, rooting through the bag as I put everything away, trying to find a spot for everything when my hand closes around something that shouldn't be in there. A gun. It's the twin of the one Jack had back at the loft, being small, sleek, and deadly-looking. Did he put it in there by mistake? No, that doesn't sound like what I've seen of Jack. I put it back hurriedly. For now, it's enough to know where it is.

I head back out into the diner, ready to eat at last, and find that things have changed a lot since I left. Jack isn't at his table, but instead has his back to the wall, held there by two of the truckers while the third goes through his pockets. He doesn't seem particularly bothered by it, but he does give me a level look as I come in.

I know what I have to do. Reaching into the duffle bag, I pull out the pistol, taking off the safety, leveling it at the guy going through Jack's stuff and trying to make my voice as even as possible.

"Back off, all of you. Do it now, or I'll shoot."

The trucker going through Jack's pockets stops, turning to face me. He starts walking forward, and I aim the gun at his leg.

"Stop," I order.

"Yeah right," the man says. "With that angelic face, I bet you're too scared to even hold a gun."

He takes another step and I pull the trigger automatically. He goes down, clutching his leg. "Dammit, I didn't think you would-"

"Tell those guys to get away from my friend right now or I'll shoot off something more important to you."

He hesitates, and I shoot him in the other leg. He cries out in pain.

"Now!" I command.

His buddies move away from Jack without being told. Then Jack does the one thing I don't expect. He takes out a wad of cash and hands it to the guy on the floor.

"Thanks. You can go clean up now."

Before my mouth can even drop open, he has a hand on my arm, leading me out to the car. "Time to go, Celes."

We're almost to the Aston when I finally get enough composure back to speak. "What was that about?"

Jack nods, taking the gun from me smoothly. "Sorry, but I had to do that."

"Had to do…" I get it then. "It was all a set up. You had me shoot someone."

"The gun was loaded with blanks. Alphonse back there just has natural theatrical talents."

"It was still some sick game-"

"This *isn't* a game, Celes." Jack's expression is earnest then. "I had to know how much I could trust you. You had a gun, and I was obviously distracted. You could have run off. You could have shot me. You didn't."

I can almost understand it. "So this was all just a test?"

"I live my life pretty close to the edge," Jack says with a smile. "All faders do. In that kind of world, multiple choice wasn't exactly going to cut it. The good news is that you passed. Not that I imagine that matters to you right now. You're still too upset with me."

That's a pretty good summary of my feelings right then. I don't know whether to hate him more or less right then for being able to predict that much about me.

"So I passed by being willing to help you?" I demand.

"That and being calm when things got tense. Oh, and you obviously knew what you were doing with the pistol. That could be useful too."

"Useful how?"

Jack shrugs. "Having skills like that are the only way you're going to get any real answers from the Underground."

FOUR

This time, there's a faint glow of light on the horizon as I open my eyes. My head's resting on something that turns out to be Jack's shoulder, which doesn't seem to make any difference to his driving, but does make me jerk awake far quicker.

"Sorry," I say.

He shrugs. "It's fine."

"Why is it that I keep falling asleep around you?"

"Must be my riveting company," Jack suggests. He has a point there. We hardly spoke after he started to suggest that I might be somehow dangerous, and a long drive with no conversation isn't exactly the best way to stay awake. "Still, we're here now."

'Here' turns out to be a patch of desert, with an old road running through it. Not the kind of place you find anywhere near home. But then, given how long we've been driving, and the speeds Jack has been driving at, we *aren't* anywhere near home.

We are near what looks to be an old aircraft hangar. The kind of place that was probably the heart of a busy airfield once, but now is just something to attract rust. It's the kind of place that, even if you saw it from a way away, you wouldn't come any closer to have a look around. It just wouldn't be worth the effort.

"This is where we're going?" I ask, and Jack smiles at the surprise in my tone.

"What were you expecting?"

I shrug. "I don't know. Something with more razor wire and guards, I guess."

"We have that inside. Out here, it would just attract attention."

That makes sense. After all, I guess nothing says 'secret government base' quite like a bunch of soldiers hanging around outside glaring at anyone who gets too close. This place doesn't look secret. It just looks... dead, like a one building version of the kind of ghost town that was doing fine until the desert claimed it.

"This is it, anyway," Jack says. "The place where you fade and get your new identity."

Those words make something tighten in me. I don't want a new identity. I want my old life back. I want some answers too. Right now, of course, it looks like the only way I'll get either is by going along with this as far as it goes. Jack drives right up to the hangar, stopping the car just outside a nondescript door on the outer wall. He clambers out of the car.

"Come on, Celes."

I decide not to argue. Better to get this over with quickly. I stumble a bit as I get out of the car-I've been sitting still for so long that my legs are asleep-but I follow Jack around to that door. It's only as we get close that I notice the sophisticated electronic lock on it. Jack has to key in a code while looking into some kind of scanner before we can step inside.

There's a corridor on the other side of the door, which swings shut behind us as soon as we step inside. The walls are whitewashed, while there are strip lights set into the ceiling. They light up as we walk beneath them, fading away again behind us. With that, it's hard to avoid the feeling that someone somewhere is watching us. Either that, or the security in this place is high-tech enough to amount to almost the same thing.

It all reminds me of some kind of military installation. The kind that you see in movies, which don't officially exist, but do always seem to have secrets lurking in their depths. The kind that are very well-protected indeed. Briefly, just briefly, it occurs to me that I couldn't leave here even if I wanted to. It's enough to make me freeze in place. Then Jack puts a hand on my shoulder and I keep walking.

There's an elevator at the end of the corridor. The buttons in it don't have any markings, but Jack knows which one we need. We head... I'd guess down,

FADE (FADE SERIES #1)

because there isn't enough of the building for us to go up that far, but it's hard to be sure. The doors open, and we step out into a circular room that is dimly lit and empty. It kind of reminds me of a movie theatre in the seconds before the movie starts, only with just Jack and me there. A second later, I find out what a good guess that is, because a movie starts playing. It's on all the walls of the room simultaneously, so that I'm surrounded by the images. I couldn't look away even if I wanted. And the weird thing, the *really* weird thing, is that I seem to be the star of the show.

    Most of them look like home movies, only they aren't any home movies I remember. We don't go in for that much in my family. Somehow, though, there's grainy footage of me as a little kid playing with my parents. There's film of me riding my bike for the first time, making a mess trying to help my mother bake when I'm only a few years old, going to birthday parties. It's like a montage of my whole life, strung together from pieces of footage I didn't know existed.

    There's even footage of me from just yesterday, when my family disappeared. Me running around the house trying to find my parents, my brother. Me calling for help. Me collapsing after the telephone call in the living room.

"What is this?" I demand of Jack. "What's going on?"

In answer, he just points up to a section of tinted glass above the section where the movie is playing. I realize then that someone is watching me even now. Someone is sitting behind that glass and... what? Making notes?

"What's going on?" I repeat, directing my question at the glass this time.

"Hello, Celestra Caine." The voice comes from speakers I can't see. It's strong, male, distinguished. "Be welcome. We have been expecting you. Mr. Simple has done a good job in getting you here safely, I see."

I nod. I guess *almost* being shot by goons back at the apartment doesn't count. That nod seems to be enough for whoever is behind the glass.

"Good, then we will proceed."

The screens change then, and I realize that they are glass panels too. They are clear, and behind them, I can see people. Some are busy at work, while others are staring through at me and Jack. At me. For a moment, I feel like something on a glass slide under a microscope. Then the voice from the speakers continues.

"Celestra, as you can see, you came to our attention some time ago." The voice sounds matter of fact, as though its owner is reading all this from some kind of file. "You were found shortly after your birth in a dumpster, without any recognizable identity."

"That's not true-" I start to say, but Jack's hand is on my shoulder again, squeezing in a way that is clearly a warning.

The voice from above doesn't seem to mind. "As I said, a police officer found you abandoned. You were given into the care of Children's Services, while initial attempts were made to find your parents. When it was clear that they would not be found, you were put up for adoption. The couple you believe to be your parents, the Caines, adopted you right away. That is to be expected. A newborn baby was just what they could have hoped for, in the circumstances. You had no history to overcome, no problems to deal with. You were just their sweet little girl."

One fragment of the glass walls starts playing the movie collection from before, as an illustration to the unseen speaker's words.

"For a long time, it seemed that you were no more than a normal girl. Maybe a little prettier than average, but nothing out of the ordinary. You had friends, you joined activities and sports at school, you were a good daughter and sister. From what we have seen, your boyfriend Grayson adores you, and your teachers, would easily recommend you for that scholarship to Georgetown University you want."

What hurts is the casual way all this is tossed out, as though none of it really matters. As though it is just a collection of observations, rather than my *life*.

"Why are you doing this?" I demand, shrugging off Jack's hand. "Why are you telling me all this? Why have you been *watching* me?"

The voice doesn't hesitate. "As I was saying, you were, to all intents and purposes, a perfectly ordinary teen. Circumstances, however, have led us to believe that might not be the case. That you are in fact much more. Are you, Celestra?"

I look up at the glass blankly. "I don't know what you're talking about."

"Of course, we have already established that you might not. Even we only know some of it, but still, taking you underground... fading you, was deemed to be the correct option. The safe option. You see, Celestra Caine, we have reason to believe you may not be from around here at all."

"You still haven't told me what's going on." I look over at Jack, hoping that he will make more sense than whoever is speaking, but he just looks back at the dark glass of the observing room above. I do the same, and as I do, the glass clears, letting me see through to where a middle aged man in a dark suit stands. He has a kindly look to him, like someone's rich favorite uncle, with hair that has just started to Gray and features that seem open and inviting. Yet there's a sense of authority that rolls off him as he stands there.

"I am Sebastian Cook. I head this group of scientists, researchers, and other leading minds devoted to research in areas that are, let us say, not entirely normal. We believe that you are very special, Celestra. Specifically, we believe that you have abilities dormant in you that could yet prove to be phenomenal."

"Abilities?" It's hard not to scoff at that. "What am I, some kind of TV psychic?"

The middle aged man's face creases into what's probably a smile. "Something like that."

"What is this? Some kind of joke?"

"It's no joke, I'm afraid." Suddenly, he's serious again. "We have only caught glimpses of what might be possible, Celestra, but until you are able to control what you can do, we will have to be very careful with you. You could potentially be a danger to many people, including yourself."

I don't like the sound of that. "It sounds like you're planning on locking me away down here."

"You already know what we plan," Sebastian Cook says.

"You want me to fade?"

He nods.

"Why?"

"Because we're not the only ones who have noticed your potential, Celestra. And we're not entirely sure others would want to keep you alive."

FIVE

While I'm still trying to make sense of what Sebastian Cook has just said, up there in his box, the glass walls around me and Jack slide away to allow through a team of men and women in sterile white clothing that makes them look like they're ready for some kind of medical procedure. I take a step back automatically.

"There is nothing to worry about, Ms. Caine," Mr. Cook says. "The people here are merely going to make it easier for you to fade. It is a necessary step to protect you from those people who would harm you for what you are."

"Who are they?" I demand, still unwilling to believe most of this ludicrous story of his. Well, who *would* believe it if someone just told them that they were meant to have some kind of special powers. Only the sheer scale of the place I'm in, and the amount of trouble that Jack has gone to over me so far, keep me from laughing at it outright. From calling it all a joke.

Because it can't be a joke. No one would build a whole military base for a joke, or send men after me with guns, or have me do Jack's "test" back at the diner on the way. I shiver as I realize that no joke would include surveillance on me for so long, or my family disappearing like that, or my phone being cut off. But that leaves only one possibility: that this is real. I'm not sure I'm ready for that yet.

"Who are they?" I repeat. Even though the people in white look friendly enough, I'm not letting them touch me until I get some more answers. I'm not some little kid to be pushed around. At least, I hope I'm not.

"We call them the Others," Sebastian Cook says. "We don't know much about them, except that they will be looking for you, and that they will not want you to live. When they found out about you... well, given how different you are, we had to act."

"That's not an answer." I see Sebastian Cook's expression darken slightly, and I know how I must sound to him. Like some kind of petulant, ungrateful child. "Look, Mr. Cook, I'm sorry. I appreciate you sending Jack to help me escape those men who went after me, but right now, I'm completely confused. Can't you tell me more about what is going on? You haven't even told me why you're so convinced that there's something odd about me."

That seems to please him, and he nods. "I can try," he says. "Ms. Caine, we have... sensors here. I guess you could think of them as a kind of radar. They detect the unusual, the different. Things that go beyond the normal in some way. Most of those signals are weak. When we intercepted yours, we thought it had to be a mistake, or an indication of some kind of forgotten lake monster. Those are large enough to put out that kind of response."

Great, so now I'm the Loch Ness Monster. I look around at Jack automatically, not knowing why it *is* automatic for me, but looking anyway. I guess I want to know why he didn't tell me this on the way, or just find out how much he knew. He stands there totally impassively, of course. No, that isn't right. Not totally impassively. He's just trying to give that impression. Somehow, I know that, if he could, he'd be comforting me right now. Reassuring me that I'm not some kind of freak.

I have to admit, that's a good thought. I don't know why it matters to me what Jack Simple thinks of me; after all, he hasn't exactly been the best of company on the way over, but it does. Maybe it's just that, in this strange place, being told these impossible things, he's the closest thing to a friend I have. Then again, maybe it isn't.

I force myself to look back up at Sebastian Cook. "So you're saying that, not only am I some kind of freak, I'm one of the biggest freaks you've spotted?"

He shrugs. "If you want to put it that way."

"No, I don't want to put it that way! I don't want to put it any kind of way! I..." I don't know what I want. I don't know what to believe. I do know that suddenly, I'm crying, and I hate it. I hate that I'm crying in front of this bunch of strangers, when I should be standing up tall and facing them down. I hate that I suddenly don't know what's going on in my life, or even what kind of life it is, given what Sebastian Cook has just said. I hate what has happened to my family, to me... all of it.

I feel arms around me. One of the technicians, maybe? To my surprise, I find that it's Jack. Just Jack, pressing me against the fabric of his suit and letting me cry on his shoulder while one hand runs through my hair.

"Hush, it will be all right. I promise."

I want to rail at those words. How can he even begin to say them when things are so very far from all right now? Yet somehow, said in those calm, certain tones of Jack's, I find myself believing them. Normally, no one other than Grayson can calm me down like that. Normally, I won't let them. Except with Jack, it just feels natural. I pull back then, unwilling to stay there with everyone watching me and probably thinking what a foolish little girl they have to look after. I won't have them thinking about me like that.

When I look round, I see that Sebastian Cook has come down from his control room, and is walking in through the glass partition.

"You're wondering exactly what you are," he guesses as he comes forward.

I nod. "I mean, you make it sound like I'm the yeti or something, Mr. Cook."

"Call me Sebastian."

I catch Jack's look there and I get the feeling that his boss doesn't allow many people to be on first name terms with him. I nod. "Okay."

"The truth is, Celestra, that we just don't know who or what you are." He looks uncomfortable at admitting that, as though the idea that he might not know everything irritates him. "That's part of why we want to help you so much. We want to find out. We also don't think that the Others should destroy someone as potentially important as you just because they let their fear of the unknown override their common sense."

"Why would anyone be afraid of me?" I ask. After all, it isn't like I've been doing anything that people should be afraid of. I've been going to school, running track, and all the things every other girl my age does. None of *them* ever gets whisked off to secret locations for their own protection. At least, none that I know of. "I'm not anybody."

"As I said," Sebastian Cook points out, "there are the readings to consider. You have to understand, Celestra, that some of those things that have produced even much lower readings have been able to do quite a bit of damage. The Others presumably assume that you would be able to do exponentially more."

"And because of some sensor result, I'm meant to be a threat?" It seems a bit like SATs. One test, and somehow, everyone thinks they know everything about you. Only I don't remember getting to study for this one.

Sebastian Cook shakes his head. "Not just a threat, Celestra. An *international* threat."

There's an edge to that I don't like. "You sound like you almost agree with these Others."

He shakes his head then. "No. I want to keep you safe. They just want to kill you. But I've seen those readings too, and we can't afford to take chances. Particularly not now that the presence of the Others will make the situation worse. Until we have some better answers, you need to fade, and you need to keep Jack near you at all times."

"Why Jack?" I ask.

"You have an objection to Mr. Simple?"

I shake my head. "No, he's good."

"Oh, he's better than good," Sebastian Cook shoots back. "He's one of our best Faders. I think you won't mind his company too much either."

He doesn't exactly wink at Jack as he says that, but he certainly comes close to it. I decide to ignore the implications. It's not like I really have time to consider them in any case, because at that moment, the people in the white outfits move forward once more.

"Come on," one of them, a woman, says. "It's time we got to work."

She takes my arm, leading me out of the room with all the glass. Since Jack is just behind us, I let her. I don't know why it should matter so much to me that he's there, but it does. The room the woman takes me to is small and brightly lit, with a large chair at its center, surrounded by all kinds of implements and mirrors. For the briefest of moments, I think that I've been tricked, and that this is all some kind of interrogation room. That's what you're meant to have in secret government bases, after all, and I'm wound so tight by now that it just leaps instantly to mind.

But then I recognize some of the things around the chair. They're the kind of things you might find in a beauty parlor, not in some hidden torture chamber. I let out a sigh of relief.

"Were you expecting something different?" Jack asks, moving up beside me.

"I..." I nod silently. "What is all this? I mean, what is it all for?"

The woman with us smiles over at Jack. "Like he'd know what half of this is for. He's all natural charm and boyish good looks."

"Why, thank you, Marlene." Jack preens theatrically for a moment, and it's nice to see behind the mask, if only for an instant. Then it's back to business as he looks at me. "They're going to change your appearance, Celes. It's an essential step in the process of fading."

"Change my appearance?" I repeat, with another look at the chair. Some of the things poised on angle arms around it look vaguely surgical.

"Relax," Jack says, and I'm surprised to find that I do. "They aren't going to do anything permanent to you, and it probably won't hurt. It certainly won't leave you looking hideous, if that's what you're worried about. Just think of it like a really good makeover, and you might find yourself pleasantly surprised."

Marlene the technician leads me to the chair while Jack stands by. He's obviously not going to leave.

"Jack's right, for once. Just sit back, relax, and pretty soon, you'll be saying hello to a whole new you."

SIX

The next part takes literally hours. Hours of plucking and teasing and dying. Hours of doing things to my teeth and my skin, hours of procedures that, while they stop short of full surgery, are clearly designed to radically change the way I look. There are never fewer than two or three of the technicians working on me at once, while at some points, there are as many as six, all far too busy to answer questions from me about what they're doing. After all, it's only my body they're doing it to, right?

My hair is the first radical alteration. They dye it, changing it from its usual shining blonde to a brunette shade that's so deep it's almost black. They know what they're doing, too, weaving in highlights and lowlights until the results look, not just natural, but spectacular. With that done, they hand me a set of contact lenses, telling me to get used to wearing them. They're brown tinted, obviously designed to disguise my natural eye color.

"Though with the identity we've chosen, it won't matter so much if someone notices them," Marlene promises. "In fact, we'll give you a couple of spare sets in different shades, and you can change them out regularly. That will keep people guessing, and they'll think it's the kind of thing someone like you would do anyway."

"What?" I start to say. "I don't understand."

By that point, though, there's one of them working in my mouth, adjusting my teeth to what he assures me will be movie star perfection. I thought they were pretty good anyway, but apparently, 'pretty good' isn't good enough for whatever they have in mind. Other people go to work on tiny imperfections on my skin that I'd never even noticed before, using laser treatments I've never heard of to get rid of them. They also hurt a lot more than Jack suggested they would.

Jack is there constantly. I'm sure there's no need for him to be, because this has to be the one place where I'm likely to be completely secure, but he never leaves my side. I guess it's meant to be comforting, and truthfully, I'm grateful for it, but there's nothing that can make some of the things they do to me in the name of changing my identity any less invasive. They even go so far as to change my fingerprints, which I didn't know was possible, making me put my hands on two pads, which burn new patterns into the pads of my skin with yet more lasers. It's probably the worst thing so far.

Kailin Gow

Not that they're trying to make things unpleasant for me. They give me plenty of breaks from it all, but those are short, and even the time away from the chair often features something just as difficult to get through. There's a whole hour spent with some kind of posture coach, for example, learning to change the way I stand and walk. Then there's the time spent being lectured on fashion, being told what I should wear and what I shouldn't. I'm as into clothes as the next girl, but the woman who goes through all this with me treats it like it's a matter of life and death.

Jack smiles grimly when I mention that to him. "It is."

I guess so, but even so, all this feels very strange. Some of it seems to have nothing to do with what I would have thought of as changing identity. I get a lesson in applying makeup, for example, learning which tones to use and which not to, learning what suits my face and what just doesn't work. It's interesting, even fun, but seriously, how does that prepare me for a shift in identity? It's almost like they want to make me look glamorous, or something.

I find that suspicion confirmed when the technicians around me finally declare themselves done with the physical side of things. I don't know whether to sigh with relief or worry about what other sides there might be, but I'm certainly eager to see the results when they bring out a couple of full length mirrors.

For a moment, I find myself wondering who that girl in them is, and who does her hair. Then I realize that it's meant to be me. It's so hard to believe that I actually stand right up close to one of the mirrors, searching for some trace of the old me in there. I can find it when I look hard, but I *have* to look hard. All those small changes they've spent so long on have added up to create someone who looks so different from me it's hard to imagine.

She's gorgeous, too. *I'm* gorgeous, I correct myself, and then feel a little embarrassed about it. Not to mention confused. I would have thought that the idea with something like this was to blend in, but there's no way the version of me I see endlessly repeated in the mirrors can do anything other than draw attention. I shudder slightly at that, thinking of what it was like even before this, when that hair of mine used to get so many glances and comments. Do I really want this? Given that the alternative seems to be being shot at, I guess I'm just going to have to get used to it.

"Don't worry," Jack says, "you'll adjust pretty quickly."

Marlene taps her watch pointedly. "Come on, you two. We still have the final stages of the fade to get through, and we don't have all day to do it."

"Yes." Jack doesn't let much emotion go with that word, but I can tell that he's not entirely happy about something. I wonder what it says that, after less than a day around him, I can read him that well?

"What's wrong, Jack?" I ask.

He shakes his head. "The last part of this process... there's something you should know, Celes."

"There's no time," Marlene says. "Now, will you two hurry up?"

She practically frog-marches me to another room, with another chair.

"There's more to do?" I ask. "Seriously?"

"Seriously," the technician says, "now, sit down please." She starts sticking electrode patches to my head, like she's planning on some kind of medical scan.

"What are these for?" I ask.

"They're for your own good," Marlene says, and before she's even finished saying it, she's managed to fasten my arms to the chair with a couple of leather straps.

"Hey! What do you think you're doing?"

FADE (FADE SERIES #1)

"Please try to relax," the technician says. "The straps are just to stop you hurting yourself while the machine works."

"And what does the machine do?" I demand.

Jack answers. When he does, he doesn't sound happy at all. "It's designed to help you adopt your new identity completely, Celes. It makes you forget your old life."

"But I don't want to forget my old life."

"What you want," Marlene says, "isn't the same thing as what you need." She flicks a switch.

Instantly, I find myself remembering things. Moments with Grayson. My mom shouting me downstairs for dinner. My brother laughing because I've slipped over in the yard. Hundreds of things, flashing past so quickly that I can barely keep up with them. Flashing past, and slipping away too.

"No."

I hear myself say it, even as I reach out for the memories. I won't let them do this. I won't let them take this from me. This is my past. This is who I am. I fight for every one of those memories, and I feel pressure building up inside me. For a moment, it feels like my head is going to explode, and then...

"Damn it! Somehow, she's overloaded the system." Marlene the technician is running around her machine, trying to get it working again.

I look up at Jack. "Please," I beg, "don't let her."

Jack looks from me to Marlene and back again.

"Please, Jack."

He nods. "Marlene, leave it."

"Leave it? How are we meant to get anything done like that? Maybe if I reroute power through the back up coils, we can generate enough to-"

"*Marlene.*"

The warning note is clear enough, and I see the woman step away from her machine. "Jack?"

Jack's features are set. "Leave it. We aren't doing a memory wipe on this one."

"But it's standard procedure."

Jack shakes his head. "Not in this case. Unbuckle Celes please."

"Are you sure?" the technician asks. "I mean, Mr. Cook won't like this. We're meant to-"

"I know what we're meant to do," Jack says. "I'll deal with any fallout from this."

That seems to be good enough for Marlene, who unbuckles me. Jack helps me up.

"Thanks," I say.

"Don't thank me yet," he says softly. "Sebastian Cook might still turn around and order you back here. If he does, I don't know what I'm going to be able to do about it."

I smile. "You'll think of something," I say, and I'm surprised to find that I actually believe it.

In the end though, Jack doesn't need to do anything more than talk to the man in charge up in his office, with me along for the ride. Although Sebastian Cook doesn't seem entirely happy about it, it only takes Jack a couple of minutes to persuade him that he has no way of knowing what I'll do to more of his machines if they try to use them, and that I'll be fine as I am. He even suggests that using the machines when they don't know what they'll do could end up harming me.

"And we don't want that, do we Sir?"

"No, I guess not," the head of the underground concedes. "Just make sure that she learns her cover identity well."

I look over at him. "I wanted to ask you about that. I mean, I'm not exactly going to fit in most places like this, am I?"

"You will with the identity we've constructed," Sebastian Cook assures me. He reaches into a drawer of his desk, pulling out a sheaf of documents. "We have all the usual things. Birth certificate, school reports, passport and so on. We've upped your age by a year, because an eighteen year old has to answer fewer questions. At Jack's suggestion, we've gone with the name Celeste Channing."

"I have to change my name?" I ask, and then realize how stupid I must sound. Of course I have to change my name. There wouldn't be much point in changing the way I look if I still answered to Celestra Caine, would there?

"It's a small enough change that I can still call you Celes and no one will notice," Jack explained. "But Celestra stands out too much. Even among models."

"Models?" I feel my brow crease.

"That's the cover identity we've picked out," Sebastian Cook explains. "You'll be the wealthy daughter of a fiercely private tycoon, trying to make it out on her own through the usual rounds of a bit of modeling, making the right connections, and so on. The details are in the paperwork. It's high profile, but it's also the last place anyone would think to look."

"So where does Jack fit into this new identity," I ask.

Sebastian Cook shrugs. "There's only one role that guarantees he'll be close to you at all times. Jack is now officially your live-in boyfriend, Ms. Caine. Or should I say, Ms. Channing?"

SEVEN

The next couple of weeks are hectic. Jack and I head up to New York, where there's an apartment waiting for us, and try to settle in. We spend some time picking out furniture, and more time wandering around, getting to know the area, walking through some of the main tourist spots arm in arm, like any couple would so soon after arriving in a new city. Jack takes me around some of the main galleries and theaters, monuments and other spots, playing his role as my boyfriend well, with only the occasional look around for potential threats suggesting that he might be anything more.

He also helps me to play my role. Sebastian Cook lands me a couple of small modeling jobs through contacts of his, exactly the way that a rich tycoon uncle might for a niece interested in that kind of career. It's Jack, though, who helps me to make the most of it. He seems to have an instinct for getting me into the right place at the right time to meet the people who matter in the fashion world, so that we seem to run into them almost by accident.

I ask Jack about that, back at the apartment, and he shrugs. "It's essential to the cover we've created. A

FADE (FADE SERIES #1)

would be model who doesn't meet the right people is probably going to attract more attention than one who plays the game well. Besides, I want you to be happy with this new life, Celes, and for that, you need to live it."

I'm not certain I understand his reasoning, because to me, it still seems that it would have been safer to hide me away somewhere rather than putting me out in front of people, but I don't complain about it. This is, after all a life I could never have dreamed of.

And it has its fun moments. Like the game Jack and I play online one night where the goal is to see who can start the best Celeste Channing rumor. We take turns working with anonymous accounts Jack has set up, coming up with ever more outlandish things about the young heiress I'm playing, while watching the rest of the city's online world to see how far each rumor runs. Jack even creates a couple of news stories and buries them deep in the architecture of existing news sites, so that it seems that I've been attracting attention for a while if anyone looks. By the end of the night, we're not only falling over one another laughing, we've also managed to create the definite impression that Celeste Channing is someone New York ought to be paying attention to.

Not a huge amount of attention, admittedly. You don't become internationally famous overnight, and I'm not sure that's even the aim with the identity we've created. But we do get invited to a party, held in someone's multi-million dollar penthouse. Whose, I'm never exactly sure, because it's the kind of party where everyone's a friend of a friend, but it goes pretty well. Everyone agrees that Jack and I make a great couple, that I'm lovely and that one or two of the more mischievous rumors Jack started can't be true. Though I get the feeling one or two people hope that they are.

That party leads to more, and to phone calls, lunch meetings, invitations to events. Even to the odd modeling job, though those turn out to be less fun than they seem. There's a lot of standing around involved, a lot of rushing around, and a lot of trying to make everything perfect for the one or two seconds needed for a photograph.

Jack is by my side for all of it, and he turns out to be a lot more fun to be around than his demeanor might have suggested back at the Underground's base. I quickly find out from all the socializing that he can dance, and that he's great to talk to. Half the time, I get the feeling that people who come up to talk to us do so just in the hope of hearing one of the anecdotes he occasionally comes out with. Like the one about spear fishing off Java. He won't even tell me if they're made up.

It's easy to forget sometimes what Jack's real role is. It's easy to forget that protecting me, even being around me, is a job to him. Then, just occasionally, he'll do something to remind me. Usually by protecting me from some of the more dangerous excesses of the party scene. Everybody seems to assume that I'll be into all the things a spoiled heiress turned model would be, whether it's casual sex, or drugs, or simply alcohol. At moments like that, Jack's on hand to explain why I'm saying no, and to ensure that people understand that I mean it. I just think it's sad that he has to.

I guess that means I'm not always everyone's idea of what a girl like me should be. In fact, a few people say it outright. After talking to me, they say that they didn't expect me to be quite so smart, or reserved, or grounded. It's obviously meant as a compliment, and I try to take it that way, but sometimes, I can't help feeling that it just says a lot about what they expect.

It also says something about how I'm fitting into my role, and that worries me slightly, because there are other little signs to go along with it. Signs that say I haven't Faded as completely as Jack and Sebastian might have hoped. Signs like always thinking of "Celeste Channing" as someone else, and having to remind myself that I'm meant to be her every time someone calls my name. Signs like never quite letting my guard down, so that I acquire acquaintances rather than making friends. If my memories had been altered, I'm sure I wouldn't have that problem. I'd just *be* the bubbly socialite I'm meant to be. It wouldn't be a role I put on and take off like I'm changing clothes.

And I wouldn't have the questions I have every time Jack and I kiss. Yes, we kiss. We're meant to be together, after all, and couples kiss. So we do, almost constantly. And they're not just chaste kisses, but tender lingering kisses, kisses that leave both of us breathless. When we're not kissing, we'll be holding hands, or Jack will have his arm around me, or any one of a dozen other things that are designed to show what a close couple we are. They're necessary for the cover we're putting out, and they reinforce the idea that it's natural for Jack to be around at all times, as he needs to be. But they are complicated.

It's not that Jack isn't a great kisser. He is. He kisses with an amazing mix of intensity and delicacy, so that for the moments when his lips are on mine it's like there's nothing else in the world. That's kind of the problem, because as much as there's part of me that wants to do a backflip with joy every time we kiss, at the same time, I'm all too aware that we wouldn't be doing this if it weren't for the situation I'm in. I shouldn't be feeling that kind of thing about a guy who is only pretending to be my boyfriend, and yet it's impossible not to.

I don't know what Jack feels in those moments. I haven't asked him. I haven't dared. At the time, it always feels like he means every moment of the kiss, yet for all I know, that's just more amazing acting on his part. When we're in public, he gets into the role of the long term boyfriend so perfectly that it's occasionally hard even for me to believe that we haven't been together for months.

Back home, back at the apartment, he's harder to read. Jack stays in character, and he insists that I do, but it's like he's far less connected to me. There aren't the constant displays of affection, but at the same time, there are just enough to keep me wondering what he really feels. Was that long slow kiss Jack gave me when he caught my hand as I walked past him on my way to the kitchen for the benefit of anyone who might be watching the apartment through a long lens? Or was it just because he wanted to?

And if he wants to, should I be going along with it? I mean, I have a boyfriend. *Had* a boyfriend, at least. I don't think about Grayson too much in the first few days, because it's all too new, and complicated, and I just don't have the head space left over for anything else, but as time goes on, thoughts of him become more frequent. They're like an itch at the back of my mind, or like a favorite piece of music playing in the background while I'm trying to concentrate on something else.

I know I shouldn't think about Grayson, but it's impossible not to, sometimes. It's not just that I loved him a lot. It's not just that I didn't get a choice in giving him up, or that I can remember every little detail of him. It's almost like he's become a symbol of my old life, and by thinking about him, I've still got some tiny portion of it I can cling onto. As long as I have Grayson, Celestra Caine hasn't been completely replaced by Celeste Channing.

Then, at a party for a movie I've never heard of, it happens. Jack has gone to get us drinks, while I talk to the star of the thing, who turns out to be a lot sweeter than the character she plays onscreen, and who seems to have latched onto me as a way of steering clear of a clutch of airheads who appear to be determined that she should join their ranks for the evening.

"Your boyfriend seems wonderful," she says.

And just for a moment, in spite of all the time I've spent playing this role, in spite of all the times I've kissed Jack, I don't get it. I find myself thinking of

Grayson, and how he *is* wonderful, and how I'll never get to tell him that again.

"My... boyfriend?"

"Jack. Celeste, are you okay? You seem to be crying."

I realize that I *am* crying, and I quickly make some stupid excuse about allergies before running to Jack and demanding that he get me out of there. He does, not even asking why once we're safely clear of the place. I don't know what the people there must have thought. That I was the usual crazy model type, I guess.

Right then, I don't care. Instead, I just know that I have to do something about this collection of unresolved feelings before it destroys me. I can't go on like this, not knowing who I am. I need some kind of closure. And for that, I know, with absolute certainty, that I need one thing.

I need to see Grayson again.

EIGHT

I get my chance a couple of days later. That probably makes it sound like an escape attempt from some kind of prison, but at the time, that's what it feels like. Getting to see Grayson means dodging Jack, after all, and he watches me almost constantly. It's not like I can just tell him that I'm going to the mall and then sneak off.

Instead, my chance comes at the start of a modeling shoot. Jack's hanging around in the studio, but it's not like he can actually be in the changing room, and it turns out that there's another door. I see that combination, and I just know that I have to act. If I don't do this now, with such a perfect opportunity, I never will. So I slip out of that door, head downstairs, and take the car. I drive almost without stopping, heading out along the highways for Virginia. Heading home.

Heading for my old high school, at least. My family wouldn't remember me even if I could find them, but Grayson will. Not that I plan to talk to him. I'm not that stupid. Changed as I am, he probably won't even recognize me. I just want to see him out on the track, and know that he's okay, and... I don't know, say goodbye even though he can't hear me, or something.

I've timed my trip perfectly, because I get to the school track just in time for practice. I slip into the bleachers, down in the corner where nobody's likely to look, and I just watch. My phone rings, the way it's been ringing for most of the trip. Jack. I ignore it. If I answer, he'll want to know what's going on and where I am, and I'll be back in that life. I'm not quite ready for that yet.

I'd forgotten what Grayson looks like when he runs. He's athletic, but it's more than that. There's something graceful about him as he strides out with the rest of the team, keeping within himself, running for distance. I could watch him forever like that. There's something wrong though. I can see it. I know what Grayson looks like when he's running well and this isn't it. He's fast, but usually, he's so much faster.

When a few of the rest of the team start to pass him, our coach even calls him on it, drawing him over to the side of the track nearest me to demand an explanation. I can't hear the whole conversation, but I hear "effort", "not yourself", and "Georgetown" clearly enough. It's obvious what Coach is saying. Grayson is running badly. Badly enough that it could affect his chances of a scholarship.

It's enough to leave him looking dejected as he walks away. It's enough to leave me feeling almost as bad. Have I done this to him? I realize in that moment that I shouldn't have come here. Seeing Grayson like this hasn't helped me to put thoughts of him aside. Instead, it has just shown me how much my leaving has hurt him.

I know then that I need to get out of there. Turn around, walk away, and get back to New York. Call Jack to let him know I'm fine. I need to do all of it. I make my way down from the bleachers and start back towards my car. It's only then that I see Grayson standing there, looking straight at me. I turn, walking quicker, but it's too late.

"Celes?"

I break into a run without thinking about it, heading out across the park near the school. It's a stupid move, I know, but right then, I simply can't face Grayson. Only I'm going to have to, because he's chasing me, and he's always been able to run faster than me. In fact, I've barely gone fifty yards before he catches up with me, colliding with me so that we both tumble to the ground in a heap.

He looks at me then, staring in shock and, I realize, embarrassment.

"I'm so sorry," he says. "I thought... I thought you were somebody else."

He doesn't recognize me. It seems that all those technicians back in the desert did a pretty good job. Yet having Grayson so close and not know that it's me is hardly something to make me happy, particularly not with the way Grayson's face falls as we both make our way back to our feet.

"I'm really sorry," he repeats. "It was just that, sitting there, walking, you reminded me so much of-"

I can't bear to hear him say my name. Not now. Without thinking, I reach up to touch his face. "It's fine," I say, even though it really isn't fine, not then. "People make mistakes."

"Even your voice..." Grayson begins, and then pauses, looking at me closely. It's like what he's seeing doesn't match what he knows he should be seeing. "Celes?"

I shake my head. "I'm sorry, I don't know who that is. I'm not who you think I am."

That hurts me just to say it, but it seems to hurt Grayson more. He kind of folds in on himself, sitting down on the grass and I want to reach out to hold him, but I know I can't.

"I've been searching for my girlfriend for weeks," he says, "and it's like she just vanished. It's not like her at all. She wouldn't just leave me a text message breaking up with me. Celes wouldn't do that, she would talk it out with me before that." Grayson shakes his head. "Something's happened to her, and I have to find out. I have to find her..."

"Gray-" That syllable escapes before I can stop it.

"What?" Grayson looks up.

"Nothing." I shake my head. "Look, I'm not who you think I am, but I hope you do move on. Whoever your girlfriend was, she's not worth moping for, if she dumped you the way you said she did. Move on, get a new girl..." I can't finish that. I know I should want Grayson to be happy, should want him to find someone who can take some of this pain away, but the thought of him with someone else just isn't one I can stomach.

It doesn't seem like one Grayson can handle either. He stands. "If you knew Celes, you would know she's worth everything to me. I loved her... so much. I still love her."

I reach out to put a hand on his shoulder, and Grayson reacts, turning it into a hug. I've missed those hugs. But when he jerks back, I know something's wrong.

"You even smell like her."

I don't answer, but walk for my car. Grayson follows. And it's then that I notice the car that's parked just a little way from us. It's a black sedan, which is unsubtle enough in itself. You'd think that people would pick something else for stake outs. The fact that there are a couple of guys in it just staring at us makes it even clearer. Someone has found me.

"Oh no. No, no, *no*."

"What?" Grayson asks.

Are they here because Jack has sent them to pick me up? He'd be able to track my phone, right? Probably even my car. Somehow though, I know he hasn't sent them. Jack would have come himself.

The two men get out of the car. They're dressed in black, the same way the men from Jack's apartment were. I try to work out which way to play this. I could run, but if they're armed, then I'll just be a perfect target. Or I can play it cool and hope that my disguise holds. That sounds like the better option by far.

I turn to Grayson. "Thank you, sir, for telling me how to get back to the highway. I guess I'm more lost than I thought."

I walk for my car then, hoping it will be enough, but I can't resist a glance back. That's when I see that one of the two men has taken hold of Grayson's wrist and is dragging him towards the black sedan.

I'm not sure about what happens next. I react purely on instinct, knowing that I have to help. I run over, grab the arm that's holding Grayson, and twist it so violently that the man yelps as he lets go. His partner's eyes widen for a moment, and he charges towards me. It just seems so natural then to move slightly to the side and push. The results of that are not what I expected. The man goes flying. Literally flies through the air, to land with a crash on the windshield of his own car.

His partner has recovered enough by then to swing an elbow at me, and I dodge back, bringing my foot up automatically, swinging it as hard as I can between his legs. He goes down, whimpering.

I reach out to grab Grayson's arm then, knowing what I have to do. "Come on, Grayson! We have to run."

"Run?"

"They'll be after you too, now."

Grayson looks puzzled. "What's going on?"

That response is understandable, but there isn't time. Already, the one I've kicked looks like he might be starting to recover.

"Come on, unless you want to face these two again. And for all we know, they brought friends. Trust me, Grayson."

That's enough to get him moving, at least. We get in the car.

"You still haven't told me what's going on," Grayson says.

I take a breath. "If you want to go back to your normal life, you have to trust me and promise not to say anything to anyone."

"Trust you? I don't even..." then he looks at me. Really looks at me. I can practically feel Grayson stripping away the layers of disguise in his mind. We don't have time. I put the car in gear and drive, as fast as I dare, wanting to put distance between us and the men behind us. We've gone maybe half a block before Grayson finally says it.

"Celes."

Maybe it's just that I'm concentrating on the road this time, or maybe I'm finally ready to give in to it, but I turn to Grayson as he says it, responding to the name.

"It is you," he says. "I knew it. I..." He leans over to kiss me, which I'm sure is some kind of traffic safety violation, but right then, I don't care. I just care about the familiar taste of those lips on mine, and that way Grayson has of being exactly what I need so that I can shut out the-

I swerve just in time to miss an oncoming SUV, and decide that there will be time for kissing him later. At least, I hope that there will.

"Celes," Grayson says, pulling back. "What's happening? Why are there people attacking you? Why did you disappear? Why do you look... like that?"
I just smile. "I've missed you too, Grayson."

NINE

I return my attention to the road after that. A getaway isn't much use if we end up crashing in the middle of it, and I'm driving too fast to do anything but concentrate. I can't drive like Jack does, with that uncanny knack he has for knowing where there are police patrols, and the ability to push the Aston to its limits, but I still drive as quickly as the traffic around us allows. I'm wound tight as I drive, glancing around constantly, looking around for any sign that Grayson and I might have been followed.

So when the black sedan pulls in two cars behind us, I spot it instantly. I almost panic then, almost floor the accelerator and just hope for the best, but I take a breath, forcing myself to be calm as I look closer in the rearview mirror. It isn't the same car as before. It can't be, because this car has a perfect windshield rather than one covered in cracks from where a body has hit it. There have to be plenty of black sedans in the world, right? It might be nothing. It might just be someone on their way back from work.

I believe that about as much as I believe that the men back at the school had just been there for something innocent. I have to act. I have to do something that will tell me straight away whether this car is following me, so at the next intersection, I take a good look at the traffic around me, grit my teeth, and run a red light. Horns sound, and brakes screech, but when I look back, I have my answer.

The black sedan hasn't followed.

"Celes?" Grayson asks. "What are you doing?"

"I'm sorry. I thought..."

I tail off as I glance up at the rearview mirror again. The sedan is still way back at the intersection, but there, two cars back again, another black car has pulled in behind us from a side street. It could just be a coincidence. It's a different make and model to the sedan, and black's a common color for cars. But somehow, I don't buy it.

I take the next turning, not caring that it sends me cutting across traffic. Again, the following car doesn't go with the move, but again, a jet black vehicle settles in a few places back a street or so later. This one is a van, which stays for about three blocks before being replaced by what looks a lot like the original sedan. I guess most people would have forgotten about it by that point. After all, who really looks at the cars behind them?

"Celes," Grayson says. "Talk to me."

There's only one conclusion I can come to by this point. "I think we're being followed, Grayson."

"Followed?" Grayson sounds like he hardly believes it, but then he takes another look at me. It's easy to guess what he's doing. He's looking at all the changes to my appearance, finally thinking about why I might have needed to make them. "Celes, are you in some kind of trouble?"

I bite my lip, weaving past another couple of cars. "You could say that. Look, Grayson, I need you to trust me for now, okay?"

Grayson nods without hesitation. "I do trust you."

I head away from the town, out onto the highways. There, I guess that I'll have the advantage. After all, I'm the one in the sports car. Once I'm on the open road, I give up worrying about what the police will think and just go as fast as I can. I figure that if the police stop us, at least whoever's following won't dare do anything with them around. I hope.

So for the next half hour, I play cat and mouse with more black vehicles than I can count. I have the speed, but it never seems to be enough. I'll power away from the sedan or one of its sister vehicles, but whenever I slow down enough to look round, there's another one, taking over the chase. It reminds me of the way I've heard wolves run down deer, pushing them towards one another, running them until they drop from exhaustion.

Of course, since I'm the deer in this scenario, I don't want to think about what happens then.

My phone rings again, and I start to ignore it. This isn't the time for an argument with Jack. Yet almost as soon as I think that, I change my mind. After all, if anyone can help me now, it's Jack. I take out my phone and answer. On the other end, Jack's voice is tense, even frantic. I don't think I've ever heard him like that before.

"Celes?"

"Jack!"

"Celes, are you safe? Does someone have you?"

It takes me a moment to realize what he means. When I do, I feel a second of deep embarrassment. With my going missing this morning, Jack actually thinks I've been kidnapped, when I've actually just gone off looking for my boyfriend. Of course, given that the black van's back on my tail when I look at the mirror again, there might still be time for his first instinct to be proven right.

"Celes?" Jack repeats.

"Jack. Jack, I'm fine." For a moment, relief at hearing his voice overwhelms me. "No, I'm not fine. I'm sorry. I know I shouldn't have done it. I took the car. I just wanted to see... to move on. I needed to visit Grayson again."

Jack's groan is audible down the phone. I know what he must think. That I'm an idiot. Worse, that I've gotten into the spoiled little princess role far too much. I'm surprised to find how much it matters to me what he must think. I don't want to disappoint him like that, and now I have.

"Were you followed?" Jack asks, his voice tight.

"That's the problem," I say.

"Oh, Celes." Another groan. "What happened?"

I explain about the cars swapping in and out behind me, despite all the things I've been doing to try to lose them. Jack doesn't seem surprised by it.

"It's the professional way to tail someone. The idea is that people will spot one car that's behind them for miles, but different cars just look like normal traffic. You did well to spot them at all."

There's a faint note of approval there that reminds me of the way Jack sounded after his 'test' with the gun at the diner. Like I've done better than he expected me to. That's why it's such a shame that I have to tell him the rest of it.

"I only spotted them because the sedan looked just like the one they used when they tried to attack me and Grayson."

"They spotted you with him?" Jack asks. "How many were there?"

"Just two at the time. I knocked one out, and the other... well, he probably won't be in great shape for a while either."

"Do I want to know how you did that?" Jack asks, and then pauses. "No, there's no time. Your ex-boyfriend is in a lot of danger now, Celes."

"I know," I say. "I'm sorry."

I can just picture Jack shaking his head. "It's too late to start worrying about that now. Tell me where he is, and I'll send a team around to keep an eye on him."

I hesitate just a fraction. "Grayson is with me, Jack."

"Okay." It's a shade of the word that doesn't mean it at all. "Where are you now? I've been able to take a general direction off the scanners, but I need something more specific."

"I..." I look up and read the next sign I see to Jack. "Jack, I'm not sure how long I can keep this up."

"You're doing fine," Jack reassures me. "You just need to keep driving, Celes. Whatever else happens, you keep driving. Don't even stop for the police. The

Others obviously know that you've spotted them, but from the sounds of it, they probably won't make a move to try to stop you until I'm there."

"Probably?" Probably isn't a reassuring word. Probably is only a step up from maybe.

"Celes." Jack's voice is suddenly firm. "I'm going to get there. You just need to hold on until I do. Do you understand?"

I bite my lip. "Yes."

He hangs up, and Grayson and I are alone again. Grayson is looking more alarmed by the second.

"Celes, I know you said to trust you, and I do, but don't you think you should tell me more of what's going on? Who was that on the phone?"

"That was..." I suddenly find that I don't want to try to explain who Jack is to Grayson. I don't know if he'll understand. I don't know what I can say to *make* him understand. "...a friend. He's going to try to help us, but from the sounds of it, it's going to take a little while."

"What about the rest of it?" Grayson asks. "Why do you look like this, Celes?"

I knew he'd ask it at some point, but how much of an answer can I give him? I don't want to tell him all the stuff about my possibly being some kind of freak, but I owe Grayson something at least.

"Grayson," I say, "I have a new identity, because my old one was in danger from men like the ones who attacked us. I can't explain everything about why, but I found out some stuff recently that means I'm suddenly very interesting to a lot of people. A group called the Underground is trying to keep me out of danger."

"What kind of stuff?" Grayson presses.

I smile tightly. "Well, it turns out that I'm adopted, for one thing. For the rest... like I said, you're going to have to trust me Grayson."

Grayson stares out ahead of him for a moment. Finally, he seems to come to some kind of decision. "Celes, whatever kind of trouble you're in, I'll be there. You can count on me. We're a team, you and I." He reaches over then to touch my face. "You've always been gorgeous to me, but now I'm seeing how gorgeous you can be. And having lost you for a short while has shown me how much I care for you. I'm not letting you go, Celes."

His hand brushes over my cheek, and I lean into the touch, sighing as I think about how good this feels. I'm so busy enjoying the sensation that I barely notice that the van behind us has been joined by a couple of sedans. When I do, my chest tightens. They're making some kind of move.

FADE (FADE SERIES #1)

I put my weight on the accelerator, squeezing every ounce of speed from the Aston Martin, and just hoping that Jack is going to be in time.

TEN

I return my attention to the road after that. And even without many other cars on the highway, I still have to concentrate hard at the speeds we're going. We're easily doing more than a hundred in places, but even that isn't enough to get rid of the cars chasing. It's not that they can catch us, but they're simply relentless. As soon as I have to slow down again, they're back.

Worse, they seem to be determined to close the gap. Where before they hung back, now the black cars come close, forcing me to push forward again and again. I don't realize what they're doing at first, because there's no way that they can catch me like that, but then I get it. Each burst forward is burning fuel, and driving like that, it's a pretty good bet that the sports car Grayson and I are in will run out of gas before their vehicles do.

I realize that the only chance now is speed. Sustained, relentless speed to leave them so far behind that they can't hope to catch up. I power along the road, overtaking cars while barely looking at what might be coming the other way, driving recklessly, even dangerously, in my need to get away. I don't know for sure what will happen if the cars behind catch up, but if what happened at Jack's apartment is anything to go by, I don't want to find out.

So I drive. I drive as fast as I can for as long as I can. I drive until there hasn't been a sign of the following vehicles for long minutes, until the fuel gauge is on the red line, and I know I'll have to start looking for a gas station soon, or Grayson and I will grind to a halt on the side of the road. We have to be safe by now, don't we?

"Celes..."

Grayson is looking behind us, and there's real fear in his tone. I know what I'll see even before I glance in the mirror, but I do it anyway. Three black cars, all sedans this time, have pulled in behind us.

They've beaten us. Run us ragged so that now there isn't any way for us to escape. The cars start to pull forward, gaining ground on the Aston a little at a time. What will they do when they catch up? Force us off the road? Shoot us without bothering to stop? I swallow nervously as I realize that, whatever they plan to do, there isn't anything I can do to stop it now.

It's at that point that I glance back again, and I see something. A flash of red somewhere behind the sedans. A second look shows that it's a sports car. A

Ferrari this time. It speeds past the sedans, and then settles into the space between us and them. In the mirror, I catch a glimpse of the driver, and my heart leaps.

Jack.

He revs his engine, and I get the message. I push my car into a last burst of speed, Jack goes with it, and the three sedans try to follow on behind, pushing up this time, their drivers apparently confident that they will soon catch us.

Then, with that little bit of space gained, Jack does the one thing they can't possibly expect. He spins the Ferrari almost in place, turning to face the oncoming sedans, and speeds straight towards them. He's playing chicken with them. On an open highway, he's actually playing chicken with three cars at once.

The sedans split, trying to go around him, and for a moment it looks like they might be able to avoid Jack, but then he changes the angle slightly, and I realize that he's anticipated their move. Anticipated it, and adjusted perfectly. He sends the Ferrari into a sideways skid, so that there simply isn't room for the sedans to get out of the way, while at the same time, Jack's arm appears at the window, a gun in his hand.

Two of the sedans swerve, trying to get out of Jack's way. There's a screech of tires as they head for the side of the highway, then one somehow clips the back of the other. It sends both cars spinning, and when they hit the side of the highway, they do more than spin. They roll.

Jack, meanwhile, is firing at the third car. It isn't a random barrage of shots. Each one seems placed, considered, which should be impossible given the speed with which the whole thing happens. The bullets aren't aimed at the sedan's passengers, but at its wheels. I see the car's front tires burst, and then it's spinning off the same way the other two did.

I don't see the next part, because I have to turn back to the road long enough to get around a minivan loaded with kids, but then Jack's new car is alongside us. I smile over at him. He doesn't smile back. I guess I should have known he wouldn't be happy, but even so, I'm glad to see him. If he hadn't shown up...

Jack points to the side of the road. I don't get it for a moment. He does it again. Finally I understand. I pull off at the next turning, which turns out to be a back road winding through farmland. Not really the kind of thing to be driving sports cars down, but we aren't driving for long. The Aston's engine coughs, and I have to drift it to the side of the road as we finally run out of gas. Grayson and I sit there for a moment, just trying to get our breath back after everything that has just happened, while Jack pulls up behind us.

When he gets out of the Ferrari, I do the same, biting my lip nervously.

"Jack..."

He grabs my arm, looking genuinely angry. "Get in the car, Celes."

It's not a tone to argue with, and it's not like the Aston is going anywhere, so I climb into the Ferrari's passenger seat. Jack gets into the driver's seat, and for a moment, I think he's just going to drive off.

"Jack, what about Grayson?"

Jack's features are taut with anger for a second. "Yes. Grayson. What were you *thinking*, Celes?"

"I..." I shake my head. "I wasn't thinking. Grayson knows."

"I guessed that." Jack slams his hand into the steering wheel. "Dammit, Celes."

He seems to get a grip on himself then. But then, Jack's always the one in control. Always the one watching over things. Watching over me.

"You must have been terrified," he says.

I hesitate, then nod. Being chased was frightening. I certainly didn't like being that helpless. I don't tell him though that what really scared me was the ease with which I managed to defeat two trained men. I shouldn't have been able to do that. The fact that I did makes me wonder exactly what I am.

Jack reaches out to touch my cheek. It's eerily reminiscent of the way Grayson touched me just a little while ago.

"You're safe now."

"Am I?" I ask. "They aren't going to stop trying, are they, Jack?"

"Safer, then."

"But not as safe as I would have been had I not come here, right?"

Jack doesn't nod. Instead, he leans into me, and for a moment, just a moment, I think that he's going to kiss me. That's a shock. So much of one that I almost pull back. He's kissed me before, so many times, but always, it's been part of the cover. It's been part of maintaining the fiction of Celeste Channing. Yet there's no one here to prove anything to. The only reason Jack would kiss me now would be if he wanted to. Does he want to? And if he does, what do I feel about that? Grayson is just yards away, after all.

Perhaps Jack senses my hesitation, because he pulls back. "Why did you even do something this stupid, Celes?"

"I had to see Grayson," I say. I know how that must sound. "I couldn't stop thinking about him. I had to... I had to say goodbye."

I expect Jack to tell me that it wasn't worth it. That I've been selfish and stupid and a dozen other things. I know all of it. Yet somehow, Jack doesn't say it. He just looks hurt.

"You passed my test. I thought I could trust you. Let my guard down with you, Celes. Let myself feel..." he turns away.

"What, Jack? What did you feel?" I ask, reaching out a hand to touch him, but suddenly I'm scared. Do I really want to hear the rest of it?

"I care for you, Celes," Jack says, turning back to me and stroking my hair. It's something he's done a lot with me in public, but here, it feels like a much more personal thing. "Probably more than I should. More than is safe."

The idea that it might not be safe to care for someone seems like a sad one. In an ideal world, Jack would just be free to feel... whatever he feels. But I know that this isn't an ideal world. Can he really keep me safe if his feelings are tangled up? And what do I feel about it? I don't know what to think. I've been playing the role of Jack's girlfriend for only a few weeks, but that's still long enough that I'm not sure what's real and what's fiction anymore. How many of the things that I'm suddenly feeling are my feelings, and how many of them are Celeste Channings?

I don't know, but right then, I do know that I want to kiss Jack. I want to do it for so many reasons. Because it feels like the right thing to do. Because we're so close already that it will hardly take anything to cover those last few inches. Because Jack looks like he wants to as well, so badly that it's almost hard not to. And because I know that, if I do, I'll know. I'll finally know whether it's an act. Whether Jack really does feel anything beyond what his role requires. Whether *I* feel it too. Here, with no one to watch, I'll know. I start to cover that last little space.

Then Grayson knocks on the window, and I remember that there is someone there to watch, and it's the one person I really *can't* kiss Jack in front of. Grayson's looking down at us with an expression that is hard to read. He moves back from the car, but I know that Jack and I will have to get out now to talk to him.

I steel myself for that. What am I going to tell him?

"What happens now?" I ask Jack, with a look Grayson's way. Jack knows what I mean.

"He's in this now, Celes. There's no going back. He'll have to Fade."

ELEVEN

We get out of the car and Grayson's waiting for us. What Jack has just said weighs heavily on me as we step closer to him, because I know what Fading means better than anyone. I know what he will have to give up. As Grayson looks at Jack, though, I know that we have a more immediate problem than that.

"Who's this?" Grayson asks, and I can hear the hostility in his voice.

"This is Jack, Grayson," I try to explain. "He's a Fader."

"What's one of those?"

Jack answers. "I'm one of the people who helped Celes to disappear, and now it's my job to keep her safe. There are some pretty serious people after her."

Grayson nods tightly, and I can't tell whether it's the situation, or simply the fact that Jack used the short version of my name. "I saw," he says, then seems to think. "So this means that Celes's disappearance... her family..."

I nod. "All down to Jack and his friends. It was the only way for me to be safe, Grayson. I'm sorry."

Grayson nods, and there's a look on his face that's hard to read. There's a touch of relief, but it mostly looks like... hope?

"So when you broke up with me, that was just-"

I move in close to him, wrapping my arms around his neck so that we're pressed together. "It wasn't me, Grayson. It was just so I could disappear."

"So you still care about me?"

I answer that with a kiss. I have far more to give it than our brief touch of lips in the car, and Grayson responds so enthusiastically that for several seconds, there's no one in the world except us. Grayson's hands slide through my hair, pulling me to him so that his lips can dance against mine. For a moment, I find myself thinking that he's not quite as skillful a kisser as Jack, but then I chide myself for even thinking that. I shouldn't be thinking about Jack when I'm kissing Grayson, and in any case, Grayson is more than good enough. There's need there, and passion, and joy.

Eventually, I pull back, laughing. It's always a good kiss when it leaves you that happy. "Does that answer your question? Now we just have to work out what to do with you. Jack can... where's Jack?"

I look around and Jack just isn't there.

He hasn't driven off, because his car's there, but there's no sign of him nearby. When I look into the

Aston, he's not there either. It's like he's disappeared. Around us, there are fields of wheat, but there's no sign of someone having gone into them, no track-ways trodden through them. Yet it's the only place I can think of that Jack might have gone.

"Jack? *Jack!*"

There's no reply, and there's still no sign of him. Then though, I catch a faint flash of sunlight off something down the road, and as I look closer, I realize it's the windshield of a car. Another of those black sedans is parked almost on the edge of sight, and beside it, I can just, *just* make out two figures struggling. Is one of them Jack?

If it is, how did he get there so fast? Grayson and I weren't kissing *that* long, were we? Yet there he is, probably more than half a mile away, struggling with a black-clad opponent. I react on instinct, starting to run towards them, knowing that I should help, even as I'm not sure exactly what I can do. Though I did okay when it came to helping Grayson.

I hear a car start behind me as I run, and I realize that Grayson has taken Jack's car as a quicker way to get there. Yet he doesn't overtake me. He's in a sports car, so he should roar straight past me as I run, yet Grayson doesn't. Even with the amount of time it's taken him to get into the Ferrari, that just doesn't make sense.

I glance back, and I suddenly feel dizzy. I'm used to moving quickly thanks to my track practice, but this is different. This is far faster than I've ever run before, so that the air rushes past me and the ground blurs beneath my feet. It's faster than the track records back at school. It's faster than the state records too. If I could run like this to order, in fact, I would probably be winning international competitions, but that thought doesn't fill me with the joy that running fast normally does. Instead, this is so much faster than usual that it's almost frightening.

It isn't long before I'm alongside the sedan where Jack is struggling with a man in dark clothing. The fighting is brutal, all elbows and knees and frantic jabs at the body's most vulnerable areas. I see Jack's opponent parry a strike aimed at his throat before kicking Jack in the knee hard enough that Jack stumbles. Yet they keep a grip on one another.

No, not on one another. On a gun. It looks like it might be Jack's, and both men have a death grip on it as they wrestle for control of it, battering one another around it as they struggle to force the other to let go.

Jack spots me then, and looks over. "Celes, stay back. Get away."

It's only a moment of distraction, but it's enough. The man in the black clothing brings his head forward in a brutal strike, then twists the gun around. I hear the dull crack of a shot.

"Jack!"

Jack stumbles back, slumping against the car as he clutches his shoulder. Blood is already starting to come from the wound, spreading out around it in a darker stain on his suit. The man who now holds the gun raises it for a second shot.

It feels like the moment when Grayson was in trouble, back at the school. It's like I know exactly what I need to do. I reach out, take hold of the gun, and twist it back towards the man. It hardly feels like I'm doing anything, but the gun turns easily, and a second later, I'm holding it. I guess the sensible thing would be to use it, but I don't. I throw it, as hard and as far as I can, so that it sails out over the nearest field and lands somewhere in that golden spread of wheat.

The man turns to me then, and I should be afraid. I know I should. Just from the short section I saw of the fight with Jack, I know that this man knows far more than I do about hurting people. He's bigger than me, almost certainly stronger than me, and he clearly has no compunction when it comes to hurting people. Yet I'm not as scared as I should be. At that moment, in fact, I'm not scared at all. I'm just angry.

If either of us looks scared, it's the man in the black clothes. It's like he can see something about me that I can't, and what he can see terrifies him. He moves forward anyway, swinging a hasty punch at me. I bat it aside easily. My hand snakes out in the moment afterward, fastening around the man's throat. For a second, he looks absolutely frantic, but then it's too late.

Heat pours up through my hand, and light flares from it, pure and white. It's so bright that it ought to be blinding, yet I find that I can look straight through it with no problems. I almost wish I couldn't. The man's features are a mask of agony as the light burns through him. He doesn't scream, but I can see that he wants to, as this flame flashes its way down his body as quick as a forest fire so that it seems he's burning from the inside out.

The whole process takes maybe a couple of seconds, but in that time I'm able to see every detail of it. Not that I want to. This is the kind of thing that I know will haunt me. The kind of thing that will show up in my dreams even after I've thought I've forgotten it. Yet even as I think that, I also find a small part of me thinking that it's a good thing. That the man in front of me deserves it if anyone does.

And then it's done. The light is finished, leaving me holding nothing more than a blackened husk that used to be a man. A few flakes drop from it in the breeze as I let go. I turn away. Grayson is a little way away, fighting with another man just like the first. I'm not sure where he's come from, but I don't have time to think about it anyway. For all that Grayson is fit and strong, he doesn't have any special training when it comes to fighting, and he's getting hurt. Even as I watch, the man he's fighting hits him hard with a series of punches. I can't allow that. I *won't* allow that.

I walk over, and they stop. They just stop, and turn, and stare at me. I can't work out what they're staring at for a moment, until I catch a glimpse of myself reflected in the windshield of the sedan. My eyes... they're glowing. Glowing like miniature suns, with that same eerie white light that consumed a man just seconds ago. I guess I should be frightened by that, but again, I'm not. It's like one of those moments you get in dreams, when you know exactly what is going to happen next, without ever knowing how you know it. Only I'm not in a dream, and what I'm about to do ought to terrify me.

It certainly seems to terrify Grayson as I walk forward. He steps back, out of my path, looking as though he simply doesn't know me. He must know that I would never hurt him, yet he still steps back. The man he was fighting, meanwhile, seems rooted to the spot. He obviously wants to turn and run, but it's like he's simply too scared. Even when I reach out to grab his throat, he doesn't fight.

Not that it would have done him much good if he had, I think, and I can't help noticing the small twinge of satisfaction that comes with that. I wrap my fingers around his neck, and the light flares out from me to engulf him, consuming him as fully as it consumed his partner. He dies without a sound.

And then I blink, look round, and realize that I'm holding the charred remains of a human being. I drop them with a shudder. Grayson's looking at me like he can't believe what has just happened, and like he isn't sure whether to talk to me or run from me.

"What...?" I begin, but then I look at Jack, and what I see there worries me almost more than anything else. Jack looks proud.

TWELVE

I just stare at Jack for several seconds, trying to work out what to think. Trying to work out what I should say. He looks so impressed at what I've done, and the idea that anyone could be impressed by my burning two men from the inside out is just so horrific that for a moment, there just doesn't seem to be any way of talking about it. There's one point though that seems obvious.

"You knew," I say. "You knew that this would happen, Jack."

Jack doesn't reply. With anyone else, I might think that's due to shock from the bullet wound in his shoulder, yet I know that isn't it. Jack isn't talking because he doesn't want to give me answers. He's keeping secrets from me.

"Is this why people are chasing me?" I demand, moving closer to where he sits against the front wheel of the car. "Is it because they know what I can do? Is it because they know I can do this to people? Answer me, Jack!"

Jack shakes his head. "You should be proud of what you're becoming, Celes, not afraid."

I turned around on him. "I didn't say that I was afraid."

"You are though, aren't you? I know you, Celes. You're afraid of what you might do to people."

I look at the charred remains of the men I've just killed. They were hurting people I care about, but they didn't deserve that. No one deserves that. "Wouldn't you be afraid?"

"There's nothing to be afraid of," Jack insists, forcing himself to his feet. "You're still you. You have a certain amount of power, but that's all. The way you choose to use it is entirely up to you, Celes."

I wish I could believe that. I wish I could believe that this was as straightforward as that, and that I was in complete control. Yet I can remember all too clearly what it felt like in the moments when I killed those men. It felt good. It felt right. How could it feel right to burn somebody alive? That wasn't me. At least, it wasn't any part of me that I recognized.

"I'm not sure it *was* me, Jack."

"Celes," he begins, "you have to trust me."

"Why?" I demand, moving away from him. Moving towards Grayson. "Why should I trust you, Jack? Do you know what I'm becoming? If you did, then that means you knew this was a possibility and you didn't warn me. If you didn't, then it means that you don't know enough to tell me that I don't need to worry. So which is it, Jack? How much did you know?"

"We knew about you being able to move faster than most people," Jack said. "We've observed that before."

"What?" that's enough to shock me into looking at Jack again. I haven't run like that before. I'm sure of it. "When?"

"Shortly before you had to Fade," Jack says.

"That's a lie," Grayson says. "I'm the one who has been running with her. I would have known if Celes could run that fast. I would have *known*."

"This wasn't on the track, boy." There's only a few years between them, so that's calculated to insult. I decide to step in.

"When?" I demand. "When have I ever run as fast as this before?"

"You had just argued with Grayson," Jack says. "About Georgetown. Do you remember?"

I do remember, then. It's like the memory is waiting just under the surface, looking for an excuse to come up. Grayson and I had both wanted the same scholarship, and for the most part, the rivalry was friendly. But once, just once, it spilled over into an argument. Grayson told me how selfish I was being, going for it when he was the better athlete. I told him he was being an idiot, and that some of us needed the scholarship more than others.

We made up the day after, telling each other how much we cared, and how stupid we were to argue like that. We promised not to fight over the scholarship anymore, and we even tried to help one another do better. Yet until now, my memory of that argument has glossed over what happened straight after it.

I remember it now. I remember going out to the track, with nobody around. I remember thinking that I would show Grayson. That I would run faster than he ever had. And I remember running. I remember running normally at first, but then it was like something else took over. Something that made it easy to go faster, and faster. Something that made it simple to smash Grayson's time, along with any record I wanted to. With the memory so fresh now, it's easy to compare it to the way I felt when I was trying to get to Jack, and I realize that the feelings are identical. Jack's right. I have run like that before.

"How..." I half shut my eyes. "How did I just forget something like that? You didn't... do something to me, did you?"

Jack shakes his head. "You know that doesn't work on you, Celes. Things would be a lot simpler if it did."

I nod. Jack's right. Things *would* be simpler if the Underground could have adjusted my memory. I wouldn't have come after Grayson, and then this whole situation would never have happened. I wouldn't have to ask questions about being able to do the impossible, because I wouldn't have done it. I wouldn't have been here, putting myself in danger, putting Grayson in danger.

Putting Jack in danger. He isn't complaining about the wound to his shoulder, but it has to be hurting him. After all, you don't just ignore getting shot, do you? And Jack wouldn't have been shot if he hadn't had to come after me to try to save me. The Others wouldn't have found me, so Jack wouldn't have needed to fight them at all. I wouldn't have needed to fight them, or to do what I did to them in the end.

"How do you know about some argument Celes and I had back before you met her?" Grayson asks, distracting me from my thoughts for a moment with his hostility towards Jack. I decide that I should be the one to explain, because I guess that if Jack is the one to give the answers, it will only make things worse between them.

"The organization Jack works for was watching me for a while before I Faded," I say.

"A while?"

I swallow, suddenly not wanting to hold this part back from Grayson. "My whole life. They've been watching me my whole life."

"You know why, Celes," Jack says. "The Underground had to investigate the signals it was getting, though what Sebastian Cook is going to make of today's events, I don't know."

I haven't thought up to then about what the rest of the Underground might think. Until then, I've been mostly worried by Jack and Grayson's reactions. It hits me that what I've done here today will almost certainly have consequences. Jack might even be replaced as the one looking after me for this.

"Will my running off really cause trouble for you?" I ask him, and I catch Grayson looking at me as I say it. He seems confused, as though he can't work out why I might care what happens to Jack.

Jack gives a kind of one shouldered shrug, meanwhile. It's obviously the best he can manage with his injured arm. "It might, but I guess he'll probably think that was unavoidable. A consequence of the situation. The part he'll be interested in is the new ability you've demonstrated today."

Kailin Gow

It's such a neutral way to put it, as though they're just marking down test results, or keeping track of my running times. Not calmly noting that I have the ability to hurt people, to burn people. To kill people.

I can't stop myself from taking another look at those bodies. They're dried out, blackened ruins. They look like the kind of thing you might get after a house fire, or in some kind of horror movie. No, they don't even look like that, but I know what they do look like. I went to a museum once where they were showing an exhibit on the Egyptians, and there were pictures of mummies dried out by heat over thousands of years. The bodies here look like those. Like they haven't been human in centuries.

Yet they have. Just a few minutes ago, these were living, breathing men. They probably had families, friends. They probably made bad jokes in their canteen when they weren't chasing people around in cars, or went bowling, or something. They were attacking me, attacking Jack and Grayson, but I just killed them. I killed them, and I didn't feel anything. I feel it now. The breeze shifts and I get a sudden scent of burned flesh. It's enough to send me scrambling for the side of the road, where I fall to my knees and throw up.

Jack's there almost instantly, holding my hair back and helping me up, even though with his shoulder, I'm supporting him as much as he's supporting me.

"It's all right, Celes. It's all right."

"No, it isn't. I'm a walking freak. It *so* isn't all right."

"No, but it will be." He says that with the certainty I've learnt to trust. "I know this is all strange for you, but we're going to deal with this. You're going to understand what's going on, I promise. I'll keep you safe."

He holds me for a moment, and then I see Grayson over his shoulder. His expression is furious.

"Hey," he says. "Unless I've misunderstood everything that's happened here, Celes didn't actually break up with me herself. That was you, right?"

Jack doesn't say anything. In fact, he *pointedly* doesn't say anything. He blanks Grayson completely, concentrating on holding me.

Grayson keeps going. "And if Celes didn't break up with me, then as far as I'm concerned, we're still together. So it should be me comforting her, not you."

Jack looks around then, and his expression is calm, but in that dangerous way he has just before things get out of control. "This is something I have to do."

"Really?" Grayson asks, then he looks at me. "Are you and this guy together, Celes?"

I start to shake my head, but then stop myself. "We have been. It's part of our cover."

"So it's not real?"

Jack steps forward. "We have bigger questions than that."

"Like what?" Grayson demands.

"Like what we're going to do with you. You obviously can't stay around Celes."

"Says who?"

"Me," Jack says, moving towards Grayson. "Celes is in danger now because of you. You're going to have to disappear, and if you want Celes to be safe, it's not going to be anywhere near her."

THIRTEEN

Grayson looks like he can't believe what Jack has just said. "You're blaming me because Celes is in danger? Like it has nothing to do with you?"

I can feel the tension between them then as Jack lets go of me to move directly in front of Grayson, too close for it to be anything but a challenge.

"Yes, I'm blaming you."

"You have no right to-"

"I have every right," Jack says, not raising his voice. "If it weren't for you, Celes would have moved on. She wouldn't be here, in danger. Celes needs-"

"Don't call her that," Grayson says. He shakes his head. "You don't get to call Celes by that name."

I'm pretty sure that I should be the one who decides that, but I don't have a chance to say so, because Jack is already speaking.

"I'll call her what I want, because I'm the one who's going to be there for her. I'm the one who has *been* there for her."

It's hard just standing there as Jack says that. I know it's true, he has been there for me, but I also don't want him treating Grayson like this. He has no *right* to treat Grayson like this, whatever he might think about my boyfriend. Former boyfriend.

It occurs to me then that even I don't know which of those terms is the correct one. Grayson and I didn't break up, so in that sense, I guess we're still together. On the other hand, I've just spent the last few weeks living with Jack. Kissing Jack. But that was just cover. It wasn't real. Except that it felt real. The situation's enough to make my head hurt.

"Being there for her?" Grayson demands. "Is that what you call kidnapping Celes? Dragging her off who knows where and putting her in danger."

"I'm the one keeping Celes out of danger." Jack doesn't back down. "And it's not kidnapping. It's protection."

"So it's protection when you get to go around pretending to be her boyfriend? Do you kiss her? How much further do you go? There's a name for guys like you, you know."

"Grayson," I say, trying to defuse the situation. Unfortunately it seems to be a little late for that.

"Watch your mouth, kid," Jack says.

"Or what?"

I can't believe that Grayson is being that confrontational. It just isn't like him. And to do it with

Jack, who is only out to protect me, just seems stupid. I open my mouth to say as much, but then shut it again, because I've just realized how all this must seem to Grayson. Here I am going around with a guy three or four years older than me after just disappearing, driving around in cars Grayson must assume belong to Jack, letting him call me by the name only Grayson called me.

He's jealous, and it's easy to see why. From where Grayson is standing, it has to look like Jack and I are deep into a serious relationship. That I've just forgotten about him, going along with this suave, confident, handsome guy and going far further with him than I actually have. He's angry, and he's probably scared too. Scared that he's found me again only to lose me. Scared that he can't compete. That isn't a good combination.

"What are you going to do about it?" Grayson repeats. It's schoolboy stuff; the kind of thing that I'd never have thought he would resort to, but I guess after everything that has just happened to him, from being chased by men in black sedans to seeing Jack comfort me, he just doesn't have many better options left.

And Jack... Jack really isn't helping.

"I'm going to forget about you," Jack says. "It's not like you're going to be around."

"Jack, what do you mean?" I ask.

Jack half turns his back to me, and his tone is less harsh. "I'm sorry, Celes. If Grayson stays with you, the Outsiders will find you through him. That, or they'll hurt him to get to you. He has to go to the Underground, and then go on from there."

"I don't have to go anywhere," Grayson says.

Jack shrugs one shoulder again. "Fine. Stay here. See how long you last. The Others don't play games."

I see the flash of fear on Grayson's face, but he covers it well, with more anger. "I'm going wherever Celes goes."

"No, you aren't." Jack says it like it's a simple fact.

"Jack," I say, knowing that it's the only way Grayson is going to be anywhere near me, "we should let him come with us."

"And what would that do to our cover?" Jack asks.

"The cover doesn't matter," I snap back. "Not compared to this."

Jack shakes his head. "It matters, Celes. You matter. And if I could keep you happy, I would, but there is no way Grayson here can come with us. You know that. He can't be in the same place as you. It's hard enough hiding you alone, without having to add your ex-boyfriend to the list."

"I am not her 'ex' anything," Grayson says.

Jack just stares at him levelly, and I'm suddenly scared. What will happen if Grayson actually tries to attack him? Jack might be wounded, but he was holding his own against trained men before, while Grayson was just getting hurt. Do I really want to watch that? I know as soon as I ask myself it that I don't. But it seems I don't get a choice.

Grayson swings a punch at Jack, and Jack sways inside it, trapping the arm one handed and using the momentum of the movement to level Grayson down to his knees. Jack's own knee is pressed against Grayson's elbow, forcing the arm straight, so that I know he could break it with just a little more pressure if he wanted to. He manages all that without ever using his injured arm, knocking Grayson down easily.

"Jack," I demand. "What are you doing?"

"I'm trying to make a point," Jack says. "This boy is a liability. He can't fight. He can't *think*. All he can do is get you killed."

"And that's why you're doing this?" I ask Jack. "That's the *only* reason you're doing this?"

I don't get an answer to that, because Grayson chooses that moment to turn into Jack and tackle him around the legs. If Jack had been using both hands to maintain his grip on Grayson's arm, it wouldn't have worked, but as it is, Jack goes down, falling as Grayson rises above him, swinging punches.

Jack covers up, but that just means that one punch hits his injured shoulder, making him cry out in pain. It's about the worst move Grayson could have made, because it means that Jack isn't holding back anymore. In less than a second, Grayson has gone from being an annoying kid to a genuine enemy, and I don't think that's a good thing at all.

Jack's fist snakes out to punch Grayson in the solar plexus, then Jack slips to the side, climbing out from under Grayson before he can throw any more punches. In less than a second, Jack has climbed around to Grayson's back, and is choking him with his good arm.

"Jack!"

Jack doesn't so much as look up as I call his name. He's too intent on Grayson. I know I have to do something before Jack chokes him into unconsciousness or worse. I move forward, tearing at Jack's arm, trying to peel it away from Grayson's throat.

"Jack, stop!"

Jack hears me this time, and I manage to pull him away from Grayson, so that Grayson is left spluttering for breath on his hands and knees as I push Jack back. Not hard. Certainly with nothing like the strength I've used before, but hard enough that he can't get past. His eyes are furious, utterly focused on Grayson.

"Jack." I reach up and grab his jaw, forcing it round so that he has to meet my eyes. "Jack, you need to stop."

It's like those words flick a switch in him, because Jack blinks, takes a breath, and nods. He walks away then. Not far. Just to the edge of the field, clearly trying to get a grip on himself.

"I'll kill him," Grayson promises, from his knees.

I go to help him up. "Grayson, stop it. Just stop it."

"Me? He was choking me. You saw him. He would have-"

"I know what Jack would have done," I say, even though I'm not totally sure that I do. How far would he really have gone? Do I want to know? More to the point, can I really claim the moral high ground when I have just killed two men? "But he was hurt, and-"

"You're making excuses for him," Grayson says. "You actually care about him, don't you?"

I shake my head quickly. "No, it's not that... it's... complicated. Please, Grayson, don't make this difficult."

"I'm not the one making this difficult," Grayson shoots back.

"You are. You both are."

Grayson looks like he wants to argue, but then seems to think better of it. He winces. "I am, aren't I? I don't mean to, Celes. It's just that, seeing him with you... knowing that he wants to split us up. That he did split us up once already..."

"I know," I say, reaching out to touch his cheek. "But I'm here now, and I'm not going anywhere."

"That's not what he seems to think," Grayson points out.

"I know," I say again, "and I'll deal with it. Now, go and wait in the car."

"Celes-"

"Please."

Grayson goes, and I walk over to Jack. "Are you okay?" I ask.

He looks surprised at that, but nods. "I'll live."

"Would Grayson have?"

He hesitates, but nods. "A good choke is the safest way to incapacitate someone."

It sounds like a line out of some kind of training manual, and I'm not sure I believe it, but I can't afford to fight over that. "Grayson's coming with us, Jack," I say.

He shakes his head instantly. "No. He can't. It isn't..."

"Safe?" I finish for him. "Is that really what this is about? Or is it something else?"

Jack doesn't answer that.

"He's coming with us," I repeat. "No, don't try to tell me that won't work, because it's what is going to happen. You're here to protect me, Jack. I get that. I'm even grateful for it, but that doesn't mean that you get to make every decision for me."

"Not even the ones where you're making a mistake?" Jack asks.

That irritates me a little. Jack is always so certain about everything.

"I'm getting in the car now," I tell him, "and since you're too hurt to, I'll be the one driving. Grayson is going to be in that car, and you can either be civil about it, or you can wait here."

He looks at me, and I guess he's trying to work out if I'm serious. He looks like he might say something, too, but then he just shakes his head, walks to the Ferrari, and gets in.

It's going to be a long trip.

FOURTEEN

We drive a little way before I realize that I don't know where we're going, so I have to cut through some of the tension in the car to ask Jack. He's looking at Grayson as I do it, but he gives me directions. They don't sound like the way back to the apartment.

"They aren't," Jack says. "We can't go back to the apartment. Not with Grayson here along for the ride."

"I've already told you that I'm not leaving him," I remind him, not wanting this whole argument to start up again.

"I know, that's why we'll be heading to the Underground. Maybe they can work all this out. Pull over at the next gas station. The car will need refilling, and there's stuff I'll need to arrange."

I do it, and Jack gets out of the car, his cell phone out before he's even left it. He heads into the gas station store, buying what look like bandages, and then heads for the men's room, presumably to patch up his shoulder while he makes his calls. Will he be okay doing that alone? For a moment, I think about going after him to help, but Grayson's there, and I know I need to talk to him more.

"We could drive away," Grayson suggests, out of nowhere.

"What?"

"We could drive away, abandon *him*, and not have to worry about whatever he's plotting in there."

He still sounds angry about the fight. I shake my head.

"I don't think I can do that, Grayson."

"Why not?"

"You saw what happened back there. I really am in danger. And I might be a danger to other people too. You saw what I did."

Grayson nods, still not looking happy. "Yes, that was..."

"Impossible," I finish for him. "But I still did it, and the Underground might be able to tell me more about why. They might be able to tell me how much of the old Celestra Caine is real, and how much is just some kind of lie."

Grayson pulls me to him then, holding me close. "Everything about you is real, Celes. You can't let them make you think otherwise. *We're* real, and we're together. We'll stay together too."

"I hope so," I say, because it's all too easy to think of the ways the Underground might separate us.

"I know so," Grayson insists. "We'll go to college together, settle down, have a future. You'll see."

It's so easy to believe him in that moment. So safe and normal, being there with him. Not least because he's my only connection back to Celestra Caine. Without Grayson, it's like she never existed.

Jack returns a little after that, takes one look at the two of us, and hops into the driver's seat of the Ferrari. Grayson and I get in.

"Are you okay to drive?" I ask.

Jack shrugs. "I'm fine. The bullet went straight through. I'll just be sore for a while, that's all."

I don't argue as he puts the car in gear. We drive for most of an hour before coming to a private airfield. It isn't big, just a couple of hangars and a runway, but it's big enough for a private jet to be sitting on the runway.

"That isn't for us, is it?" I ask.

Jack nods. "I would have brought you this way last time, but Sebastian was using his jet."

The steps up to the jet are down, and a young man in a simple uniform comes down them. He takes the keys to the Ferrari from Jack, promising to take it back as the three of us go aboard. Even Grayson seems impressed with the luxury of the interior. This isn't some bucket of bolts bought cheaply to do a job. This is more the kind of jet that a rock star might own, complete with cabin crew.

"This all seems..." I don't know how to finish it, and for the first time today, Jack smiles.

"Most of the people in the Underground like the finer things in life, especially when it comes to hi-tech toys like this. It's one way of attracting some of the best brains out there, though plenty of them are just happy at the chance it gives them to uncover the truth."

The truth about things like me. Jack doesn't say it, but the words hang between us.

Surprisingly, he keeps away from us on the flight. Grayson sits right next to me, as though afraid to let me get too far away again. Jack, however, seems to be content to talk to the plane's crew, and spends a large amount of the flight making calls. It seems that he's busy arranging something, or reporting on what has happened. He even pulls out a laptop from an overhead locker at one point, working on it with a look of complete concentration.

"So," Grayson whispers to me, "all these people work for this 'Underground'?"

I nod. "I guess so."

"With resources like this, it has to be ex-government," he says.

"What?"

"It makes sense. What if it's some kind of renegade operation? Something that kept going after it was meant to have been shut down thanks to cutbacks?"

I shrug. It makes a kind of sense, but there are other options. "It could just be privately funded, with some big backers behind it. I think I might already have met one."

Grayson reaches out for my hand then, and I know that whatever the Underground is, whatever happens with it, I won't be alone. Jack, meanwhile, is down towards the front of the plane with one of the female cabin crew. His shirt is off. I've seen him like that before, of course. I lived with him for weeks. Yet now, I can't seem to take my eyes off him. He is magnificent, with perfectly chiseled abs and lean muscles in all the right places, although he's sporting a shoulder wound. The flight attendant is helping Jack to re-dress his shoulder, and being quite enthusiastic about it. No, it's more than that. She's practically throwing herself at him, tossing her hair, smiling at all the right moments, and taking every excuse to touch him.

Worse, Jack seems to be flirting in return. A couple of times, he says things that make the woman laugh, while he seems to be perfectly happy with her attentions. Jealousy rises up in me like a wave, and even though I have no right to it, sitting there with Grayson, I know I can't just sit there.

"I need to go to the restroom," I tell Grayson, before getting up. Of course, the path to the restroom just happens to take me right past where Jack and the flight attendant are currently finishing up. I give her a not too friendly stare. "Could you fetch Grayson a drink please?" I say. "He was complaining of being thirsty."

The woman smiles, and I feel a little bad about the hostility. "Of course."

She hurries off to fetch it, leaving me with Jack, who seems faintly amused by the whole thing.

"What brings you here?" He asks. "Bored with your present company?"

"No." I shake my head. "But I did want to see how you're doing, and to thank you for coming back for me. I know I don't deserve your help after ditching you like that to go find Grayson, but thanks anyway." This close, I can't help wanting to reach out to touch Jack's bandaged shoulder. It's probably not something he'd want, though. Not when it would only hurt more.

Jack shrugs. "You don't have to thank me, Celes. It's my job."

"Your job."

"Nothing more, nothing less."

I bite my lip. I wasn't expecting that. Not after all the time we've spent together. I really thought... I don't know what I thought.

"But-"

Jack cuts me off. "Celes, I came back for you because I had to. You're too valuable to the Underground to let go, and sooner or later, no matter how good you are at hiding, the Others would find you. You need protection from The Underground."

I can hardly believe that. It's such a cold reason. "And that's the only reason you came back for me?"

Jack draws in a breath, but he nods.

That hurts. That hurts almost worse than all the rest of it put together. "So all those weeks of pretending to be my boyfriend... You really didn't feel anything? It was just an act?"

Jack shrugs, but the movement isn't as casual as it should be. "What did you expect? That was the mission, Celes. I'm sorry if you thought it was more."

I shake my head. "No, I don't believe it. What about the kisses, the soft touches, the moments when we were all alone?"

"What can I say?" Jack says it coldly. "I'm a good actor."

I have to struggle not to cry then. "It was really just an act? Jack, please don't do this."

Jack looks away. "It was really just an act."

"Then you should win an Oscar." I can't keep the bitterness out of my voice. "You had me fooled."

I turn to walk away and go back to Grayson. This would all have been so much simpler if I had just stayed next to him in the first place. Then I feel Jack's hand on my arm. He turns me back to face him.

"Celes." It's barely more than a whisper.

"What?"

Jack takes another breath before folding me in his arms. He kisses the top of my head chastely, gently, before moving his lips down to my ear.

"I don't want anything to happen to you," he whispers, "but you have to know this. I can't afford to get involved. When we get to the Underground, they may give you a new cover. If they do, I'll be reassigned. You'll get a new Fader. One who can keep you safe."

"But what happened today wasn't your fault!" I protest. After all, that's why they'd have to change things, isn't it?

Jack shakes his head. "It doesn't matter," He says. "I'm responsible for you, and you almost got killed on my watch. Grayson almost got killed."

Despite everything Jack has said, I feel terrible. "I'm so sorry," I say. "I didn't mean..."

"I know," Jack says. He's silent for several seconds. When he does speak, there's something else in his voice. "Celes, I asked you to trust me, I told you that I would protect you with my life."

"Jack, I..."

Jack kisses me then, giving the lie to everything he has said about not caring. It's a brief kiss, but there's real passion in it. It isn't pretend. It can't be.

"I made you that promise," Jack says as he pulls back, "and I'll keep it. I'll protect you, no matter what happens. I'll protect you even if I'm reassigned. Even if I'm ordered not to."

"What do you mean?" I ask, stunned by this sudden change of tack.

Jack grins an almost boyish grin. "I mean that you aren't going to get rid of me that easily, Celes."

FIFTEEN

When the jet finally lands, on an airfield so similar to the first it's hard to tell if we've gone anywhere at all, there's a car waiting for us. It's a big, battered looking thing, but that just means it matches its driver, who's huge. He's built like a football player, and looks like the suit he wears is uncomfortably small. When Jack sees him, he raises an eyebrow.

"Louis? You're here to drive us?"

"That's right." The man's voice is almost unnaturally deep.

"There's no need," Jack says. "I can do it."

"Instructions," the big guy replies.

Jack looks uncomfortable, and takes out a phone. "I'll call Sebastian. Get this sorted out." He jabs a number into his phone. "Sebastian, it's Jack. Yes, we're here. Yes, he's met us. There's really no need... yes, I understand, but... yes, sir."

Jack hangs up, and it's clear that the big man is driving us after all. We get into the car, with Grayson and me in the back, while Jack takes the passenger seat. The driver, Louis, doesn't say much as he rolls out of the airfield. Now it's clear that we're close to the Underground. There's desert around us, and the roads are very empty. We drive for a little way before Louis brings the car to a halt for no apparent reason.

"Need to take a leak," the big man grunts, and gets out of the car, striding off a little way. To my surprise, Grayson decides that he needs the same, and heads off after him.

That leaves me with Jack. We haven't spoken much after the kiss on the plane, and I'm not sure I know what to say. Things are obviously going to change now. If we're going to the Underground, anything could happen. I might not see Jack again. If their memory device works this time, I might not even remember that he exists.

Jack seems to sense that this might be our last chance too, because he moves around from the passenger seat to join me in the back. He pulls me to him for a quick kiss.

"I've always enjoyed this part, Celes," he says. "I wasn't supposed to, but I have. And that could be a problem. I've come to care for you more than I should. It's as though we've always belong together. It sounds stupid, but I feel as though I've known you before, that we've spent centuries together, always together."

It doesn't sound stupid. In fact, it sounds perfect. I lay my head on his chest. "I know. Me too, Jack." I smile up at him. "Maybe it will work out. Maybe you'll still be a part of my life somehow."

"I know, I..."

"Help!" I recognize Grayson's voice instantly, and I'm out of the car before I even realize it. Jack's out there too, probably from the urge to follow me more than from one to help Grayson. I sprint over in the direction Grayson and Louis have gone, and quickly find them. What I see makes me recoil.

They're struggling, with both of Grayson's hands locked on the big man's wrist. In that hand, Louis holds a knife. He isn't striking Grayson, just pushing that knife inexorably forward.

Even Jack seems shocked by that. "Louis? What are you doing?"

The driver looks disgustedly at Jack. "That's exactly what I want to know with you."

Grayson takes advantage of the momentary distraction, kicking out at the driver. "Don't listen to him. We have to get him before he takes us to that place. You know what they're going to do there? They're going to erase my memories of you, Celes!"

That possibility hadn't occurred to me. I had thought about what might happen to my memories, but not about what the Underground might do to Grayson. For now though, there's the more immediate question of a man who's trying to kill him.

"Jack, you have to stop this," I say, but Jack is already moving. For all that he doesn't seem to like Grayson much, he doesn't seem willing to stand by and let him be stabbed. He pulls his pistol out from the inside of his jacket, and presses the muzzle of it to the big man's skull.

"Drop it, Louis, or I drop you."

"You should be putting a bullet in *him*," the driver says.

"Oh, for-" Jack brings the butt of the gun down sharply on the back of the man's head. Despite his size, he collapses into unconsciousness without a sound. When Grayson starts to reach down for the fallen knife, Jack kicks it away, giving him a hard look. "Don't even think about it. If you want to come along with Celes, you behave yourself, or you're getting off right here."

That's enough to get Grayson to calm down. Jack sends him to wait in the car, not taking his eyes off him until he's there. Then he searches the driver's pockets, digging out the keys to the vehicle before putting away his gun and hooking his hands under the man's arms.

"Could you give me a hand here, Celes? I'm not leaving Louis out in the desert. Not when I don't know what's going on."

Together, we just about succeed in dragging the man back to the car, putting him in the trunk. It seems like the safest place, when we have no easy way to tie him up. Jack drives. It's almost another hour before the familiar bulk of the Underground's building comes into view. We pull up outside it, and I look over to Jack.

"So, what now?"

The answer to that comes in a matter of seconds, as men and women armed with a variety of automatic weapons move to surround the car. Jack looks shocked, but raises his hands instantly. Grayson and I follow suit. They pull us from the car, and quickly disarm Jack before helping the now conscious Louis from the trunk.

"What's going on?" Jack asked. I notice that the guns are still trained on us.

The big driver clutches his head. "Maybe if you'd listened instead of knocking me out, you'd know."

At that point, one of the people with the guns radios back to say that everything is under control, and the door to the Underground's base opens, letting Sebastian Cook out into the sunlight. He blinks in it, as though he's been inside for a while, before looking over at Jack.

"Mr. Simple, I would have thought you might have handled this better."

"Handled what better, sir?" Jack asks. "Is there something I'm missing here?"

The Underground leader nods. "Oh, I think we could say that. There's a problem, Jack."

"What kind of problem?"

"That kind of problem," Sebastian Cook says, pointing at Grayson. "Ms. Caine's ex-boyfriend."

"Current boyfriend," Grayson says.

"Ex-boyfriend." Sebastian Cook gives him a look that says quite clearly that Grayson shouldn't speak, and gestures to a couple of the gunmen. They take hold of Grayson, and Mr Cook returns his attention to Jack. "What were you thinking of, bringing *him* here? You should have left him."

"That's my fault," I say, not wanting Jack to get into trouble. "I brought Grayson into this. And we couldn't just leave him behind. The Others would have killed him."

Sebastian Cook laughs. Actually laughs. "Killed him? Hardly. He's one of theirs, after all."

"One of..."

"He's the son of one of the Others," the Underground leader explains.

"No." I shake my head. "He can't be."

"Why didn't I know this?" Jack asks. "Why wasn't I told about the possible connection before fading Celes and her family?"

"It was very well masked. Grayson here may not even know it himself, but he has always been kept close to Celes. His family moved in near her family, they attended the same schools, went to the same functions. Of course, it was all designed to get close to Celes, and find out what she is."

Grayson struggles then, bucking against the men holding onto him. "That's not true."

"Then who does your father work for?" Sebastian Cook demands.

"He's just a chemist at the lab."

"A lab that is run by the Others, young man."

Grayson looks over at me, his face imploring. "Celes, I had no idea."

I find myself looking at Sebastian Cook, hating myself for not just trusting Grayson's word.

"It's plausible," he says. "Even likely. There would be no reason for them to tell their son."

Grayson pulls at the grip of the men holding him again. "You don't understand. I would never do anything to hurt Celes. I ran off with her just now, on my own, my parents don't even know. It's my choice to be here with her."

"I'm sorry," Sebastian says, nodding to the Faders next to him. "They're probably tracing you now. It's simply a matter of time before they make their way here, too. As such, the only way you're leaving here alive is if we Fade you, the way we did with Celestra's family. That will of course mean that you retain no memories of her."

"No!" The word is out before I can stop it. "Please don't fade his memories. They're the only thing connecting me to my own life."

I expect Mr. Cook to tell me that's the point, but instead, he looks almost sympathetic. "It's for both your good and his. If we don't do this, he and his family will harm you. And until we can understand how to control your abilities, you may end up harming them, not intentionally, but in self-defense."

He gestures again to the Faders holding Grayson. They start to move him away, but this time he breaks free of their grip, running over to me.

"I won't ever forget you, Celes. My heart will know you even if I don't have the memories."

I try to hold onto him, but it's not enough. The Faders pull him away.

"Please don't hurt him," I beg.

Sebastian pats my arm. "He will be the same as always, but he will only remember you as someone he's seen once or twice before. Maybe at the store, in the park..." He shrugs. "He's one of the Others, whether he knows it or not. Understand that the fact that he's being allowed to walk out of here alive and unharmed is a major concession on our part. We normally kill the Others whenever we can. Only the fact that you care for him has changed that, and with everything you can do, you're interesting enough to be worth that concession. Just be grateful that we can at least wipe his memories. If we couldn't, even that wouldn't have saved him."

I force myself to nod, in spite of the cruelty of what Sebastian Cook is saying. I can feel the blood draining from my face at the harshness of it. What worries me even more is that Jack looks every bit as pale as I do.

SIXTEEN

We go into the Underground's base then, following the route we took before along the corridor and then down in the elevator towards that circular viewing room. Grayson has been taken on ahead, so that there is no sign of him, while the guards wait in the corridor. Once we get into the elevator, it's just me, Jack and Sebastian. The middle aged head of the Underground puts an arm around Jack's shoulders.

"I know this has been a hard assignment for you, Jack. A really difficult situation towards the end, in particular."

"It's been fine."

"It has," Sebastian says. "You've handled this well. Very well, in fact. Especially given everything you must be feeling towards Celestra here."

Jack looks at the other man sharply, and I do the same.

"What has Jack said to you?" I demand. It's the only way I can think of that Sebastian might know about what Jack and I might or might not feel towards one another. If Jack *has* said anything... well, I don't know what I'll do. I just hope that he hasn't, that's all.

Sebastian shakes his head. "Jack doesn't have to say anything when it comes to this. I can guess. You're both feeling connected somehow, correct? Like you know one another?"

The elevator comes to a halt, and we step out into the viewing room. The walls are clear, letting us see that there's no one about. Compared to how busy the watching galleries were when I first came here, it's eerie. Apparently, the Underground leader wants privacy for this part.

"You know that there are things you don't remember?" Sebastian asks Jack.

"I know that you've Faded me before." Jack doesn't sound comfortable about it.

"It was necessary," Sebastian assures him.

"For the job, I know."

I have the feeling that I've walked in on an old argument between them. One that has lost most of its force, but which is still there under the surface, waiting to bubble up. The Underground leader shakes his head. "For more than that. Much more."

Jack looks like that isn't the answer he's expecting. "More? Yes. I know that I feel something around Celes that I haven't felt around anyone else I've Faded."

"What's going on?" I ask, adding my voice to the mix. I figure I have as much right to know as anyone, given how close Jack and I have gotten in the last few weeks.

Sebastian Cook stands there, his features tight. "I can't tell you that. Doing so would cause too much pain." He looks at Jack. "I'm sorry, son."

Son? "Hold on," I say, "Jack's your..."

Jack nods. "He's my father, but that isn't important right now."

"Then what is?" I ask. How can it not be important that the leader of the Underground is Jack's father? More to the point, what could be so important that it makes a detail like that irrelevant?

Jack looks at Sebastian evenly. "The memories I had of Celes are locked away somewhere, right? We never get rid of them completely. We always keep copies."

"Yes," Sebastian said. "They're in with all the other memories we've collected."

"So, in theory..."

"You know you can't go after them, Jack."

I can't help thinking of Grayson's memories. Soon, they'll be stuck in a jar somewhere, or on a computer file, or however it is they store them. All his memories of me, gone, just like that. Just like *Jack's*. Did Jack really have memories of me once? Is that even what Sebastian is saying?

"Why can't Jack have his memories back?" I ask.

"It would cause too many problems," Sebastian says, adjusting his suit uncomfortably. "There would be unhappiness as a result, at the very least. There might even be enough anger to spark violence, given some of the things there. It isn't a risk we can afford to take."

"Not that it matters to you either way," I say, suddenly angry. "You're just determined to get rid of every memory of me, aren't you?"

Sebastian looks at me, and it's the look he gave me the last time I was here. The one that says I am just a little girl who can't possibly understand the big picture. It doesn't make me any happier now than it did then. If anything, it just makes me angrier.

Jack moves over to me, but I push away from him, thinking of Grayson. Thinking of how Grayson soon won't know me. Of how soon, the only evidence that we were ever together will be in my head. There will be nobody else in the world to say that I didn't imagine half the closest moments between us. Nothing but my memories, and a few files deep within the Underground.

Jack moves close again. He obviously knows exactly what I'm going through, because he holds me close, kissing the top of my head. "It's going to be all right, Celes," he promises.

"No," I say, "it isn't. I'm not sure it ever was." I look up at Sebastian Cook. "Are you going to take Jack's memories of me too? Are you going to make it so that only you and I know I even exist? Or are you even going to wipe *your* head clean?"

"Don't be melodramatic," the older man says.

Jack obviously doesn't think it's over the top, though. "Dad," he says, moving between me and his father. "Please don't take my memories of Celes in these last few weeks. I couldn't stand to forget her."

That's a clearer indication of how he feels than almost anything he's said to me before. It seems to have some effect too, because Sebastian moves forward and pats him on the shoulder in what is obviously intended to be a comforting gesture. It might even have worked, had it not been Jack's injured shoulder.

"Who says we're doing anything to your memories of her?"

"So you aren't?" Jack asks. "You aren't planning to Fade me again?"

Sebastian shakes his head. "In fact, we want you to continue with the Jack Simple and Celeste Channing cover. It's still solid enough to work, in spite of everything that has happened today."

I wonder if he would have been as accommodating had he decided that the cover identities wouldn't work. Of course he wouldn't. He'd have had Jack whisked away as quickly as he took away Grayson.

"Besides, your presence seems to have had a beneficial effect on Celestra here. Her abilities have advanced remarkably since you came into the picture. In fact, if the outline of the situation you gave me during your flight is correct..."

"It is," Jack assures him.

"...then it seems likely that Ms. Caine's feelings towards you were a catalyst for what happened when the Others' agents attacked you."

"I'm responsible for that?" Jack asks. I expect him to look horrified at the thought, but instead, he looks almost proud.

"Not directly," his father replies, "but you helped. As such, I think it's very important that you remain around her for now. Who knows what else you could unlock in her?"

"I'm right here, you know," I point out, slightly annoyed that Sebastian can talk about me like I'm no more than a lab rat that happens to be doing well. He doesn't seem very ashamed, but Jack does.

"Sorry, Celes."

"It's okay," I say, "but right now, I don't care about all this. I want to be with Grayson. I want to know that your people are treating him okay."

"They won't hurt him," Sebastian says, as if that's all that's important. "After the memory wipe, he'll be fine. For now, he just has to wait in a secure area until we have the machines set up. It can take several hours to prepare."

"Then I want to be with Grayson until it happens," I say. Apparently, no one has thought about what it must be like, waiting hours to have your memories taken. "He shouldn't have to be alone, not knowing what's going on."

Sebastian nods. He probably thinks he's being generous. "That can be arranged."

"Then please take me there." I look around at Jack. I can guess how it will hurt him, with me wanting to go to Grayson just as we're both finding out more about his memories, but it's where I have to be right then.

"I'm sorry, Jack," I say, "but I can't just abandon Grayson after everything we shared together."

"I know," Jack says, but he doesn't sound happy about it. I think some part of him is hoping that I'll forget Grayson as quickly as he's about to forget me. That, however, is never going to happen. "I don't think I can come with you though, Celes."

"Why not?" Sebastian asks. Apparently, he genuinely doesn't get it.

"Dad, do you think I want to be in the room while Celes and Grayson say goodbye?"

Sebastian laughs. "This is stupid. It's obvious that Ms. Caine and the boy are not meant for one another, what with him being one of the Others. You, on the other hand... you're even her kind."

"My kind?" I ask, picking up on the words.

Sebastian looks a little uncomfortable, as though he's said too much, but he clearly decides that it's too late to back away from the issue now.

"You know, of course, that you cannot be human. Seventeen year old human girls do not do the things you do."

I nod, trying to play this cool. "I'd guessed."

"Jack isn't human either." He leaves that hanging for a moment before going on. "You are, broadly speaking, the same kind of creature. The only difference is that Jack had a human mother, whereas you appear to be a full-blooded example."

Jack tries to pull me to him again as I stand there in shock. "Come on, Celes. This can wait. You need to go see Grayson right now."

For a moment, I'm tempted. It would make things so easy. Just go see Grayson, put the whole thing out of my mind, and try to pretend that I haven't just been told that Jack is almost as much of a freak as me. That I haven't just been told...

I grab Jack and push him back against the nearest of the glass walls easily.

"You've lied to me Jack! All this time, you've been lying to me. You've been just like me, you've had some kind of connection to me, and you haven't said anything."

"I'm sorry," Jack says.

Sebastian has more to say. "Jack was sworn to secrecy, Ms. Caine, and here in the Underground, that is something we take seriously. He couldn't tell you. In any case, he wouldn't have known all of it. I imagine the feelings of a connection to you only came up once he was paired with you."

Jack nods. "That's right, Celes. I never meant..."

I don't find out what Jack never meant, because at that point, he slumps into unconsciousness. At exactly the same moment, meanwhile, images start to flash across the screens around us.

SEVENTEEN

Scenes flicker over the walls of the viewing room in flashes, barely giving me enough time to see any of them properly before they move on. The perspective seems odd, until I realize that the view is from someone's eyes. Jack's? He's slumped against one of the walls, and when I peel his eyelid up to check that he's okay, his eyes are flickering back and forth, the way people's eyes do in deep sleep.

On the screens around us, images of a modest house in a quiet neighborhood flash past. It's not anywhere I know, but it looks homely, even comfortable. I spot Sebastian several times, though he looks younger in the images. Young enough that Jack can't have been more than a small child. There's a woman too. She's beautiful, with eyes that are almost lavender. For a moment or two, there is nothing but the image of her smile spread across the screens.

"What is this?" I ask, turning to Sebastian. "More surveillance?"

He looks worried. Very worried. "Somehow, Jack is interfacing with the viewers. These are his memories." He shakes his head. "We shouldn't be here."

"I'm not leaving him," I say, and images continue to go past.

There's a birthday cake, with six candles on it, and a back yard, where a group of kids is singing *Happy Birthday*. The candles flicker out, and I know Jack must have blown them out, while Sebastian and the woman from before are looking on proudly.

"Who is she?" I ask.

Sebastian looks away. "His mother."

The scene flickers, and I see Jack holding a model airplane, pretending to fly it around a room. Then he's on a bicycle, riding with Sebastian looking on. Then he's in a kitchen somewhere with his mother. The images are coming too fast now to keep track of, so that I only get fragments of things. Snapshots of Jack's life.

Maybe Sebastian's right. Maybe I shouldn't look at this. Some things are too personal. Yet I know I can't look away. Not when there's a chance to finally know the mysterious Jack Simple fully. Years flash by in moments on the screen, and I can't help watching, no matter how much I tell myself I shouldn't.

"We need to wake him up," Sebastian says.

"What if it hurts him?" I ask.

"It won't hurt him as much as letting this keep going will."

I hear the fear in his voice then, so I kneel to shake Jack. I know I'm too late when Sebastian groans.

There's a door on the screens; the front door to that cozy little house. It opens to reveal a man dressed in black, and my stomach tightens in recognition. One of the Others. A man's voice asks if Sebastian is home, and the woman from before answers that he isn't, but that the man can come back later if he wants.

He doesn't wait that long. Instead, he forces his way inside, putting his shoulder to the door. Jack's mother tries to stop him, struggling with him, and it's then that I see the gun. That Jack sees it.

"Run, Jack!" The words come out clearly over the hidden speakers.

There's a panicked blur of images as the young Jack does it, but he pauses as the house's rear door, looking back. In that moment, the sound of a shot is all too clear. It's followed by something even worse: a bright, bright light I know only too well.

There's another image of the hallway then. Jack must have gone back. I wish he hadn't. However old he was at the time, no child should have to see the images on the screens right then. No child should have to see his mother with blood staining the front of her clothes as she lays on the floor, or the blackened husk of her attacker, burnt beyond all recognition. I hear the sound of sobbing coming over the speakers.

The younger Sebastian's there then, though I don't know if it was instant, or if Jack's memories have simply shifted again. Sebastian's kneeling over his wife, his hands on the ruins of her chest, trying to stem the bleeding. She looks up at him, then over at Jack, and she whispers something. It doesn't come out over the speakers, but that doesn't matter, because behind me, Sebastian says it even as she does.

"I love you both."

There's another flare of light, and as it passes, Jack's mother is gone. Completely, utterly gone, without a trace of her.

Jack... the images are confused then, and the noise from the speakers is almost unbearable. He's distraught, in a way I've never seen. I've seen people grieving before, but this is like all of them put together. Even given the weird, impossible viewpoint, this seems like sadness on a scale that threatens to spill over into madness.

There are more fragments of things. Jack in a car, barely raising his head to look outside. Corridors. Some kind of laboratory, where Sebastian is discussing something with an unseen man.

Kailin Gow

"Are you sure about this, Sebastian?"
"What else can I do? What happened... it's destroying him. This is the only way. What is my research for if not for this?"
There's an image of Jack sitting in a chair then. One I recognize, because I've sat in it too. The Fading machine. The one that takes memories. I see Sebastian sticking the electrodes to his own son's head, and I turn to him.
"How could you?"
Sebastian looks grief stricken. "How could I not?"
The memories continue. Jack learning how to cook for himself. Jack taking lessons in the martial arts, facing up to bigger, stronger boys and initially getting pounded, only for later memories to show him winning easily. Jack winning some kind of shooting tournament. It's like, even without the memories taken from him by his father, he was still driven to somehow make up for the loss of his mother. For that one moment when he couldn't protect her.
There are fewer and fewer memories of Sebastian. Instead, there are images of him locking himself away in his study. Of Jack waiting for him to come home. Of blank spaces at school sports' days where he should have been. Compared with those early memories, it's almost like Sebastian doesn't exist.

FADE (FADE SERIES #1)

"I threw myself into my work," the head of the Underground supplies. "I wanted to understand all the strange things that happen in our world, and I found myself spending more and more time with those who seemed to be able to supply real, provable answers."

"At the expense of your son," I say, looking at the screens, where there are images of Jack enrolling in the Underground, and of Sebastian, even then having meetings that he has to attend. Things he has to do away from Jack.

"He knows how proud I am of him," Sebastian says, "and I needed to find out about the man who attacked Evaine. About the abilities she demonstrated when she died."

I want to ask him about whether he thought about what Jack needed. About how he could just cut himself off like that. Yet I know I can't. That's between Jack and his father, and Sebastian will never listen to me, regardless of what I tell him. He'll say I'm too young to understand.

The memories seem to be slowing down now. Instead of coming almost in a blur, there are spaces between them where nothing happens. They jump about more too. There's Jack throwing a kid twice his size effortlessly. There's him stepping back from an alley the moment before one of the Others bursts out of it, leaving Jack plenty of time to put a gun to his head and pull the trigger. There's one that seems to be from childhood again, of Jack looking up at a dinosaur skeleton in some museum.

And there's one of him kissing me. Maybe Sebastian is right. Maybe there are some things that are too personal. Some things that shouldn't be projected onto giant screens. I reach out for Jack.

"Do you think he's any closer to waking?" I ask.

Sebastian shrugs. "I don't know. This shouldn't be happening."

I decide to try shaking him, just gently. With the memories coming slower, it should be like waking from sleep, shouldn't it? Who am I kidding? I don't know enough about science for that to be any more than a guess. I do it anyway, though.

And, in the instant that my hand touches Jack, a new memory comes onto the screen. There's a woman holding a baby. Not his mother. A different woman. She's running, and people are chasing her. For a moment, I think that they must be the Others, but then I see that they aren't dressed in black. Instead, they're dressed...

The image fades as Jack's eyes flicker open.

"Jack?" I say it softly. "Are you okay?"

"I..." Jack shakes his head. "I don't know. What happened?"

"You passed out," I say. I move to help Jack to his feet, but he's strong enough to stand on his own. "And there were images on the wall..."

"Memories," Jack says, "I remember."

I look around at Sebastian. So does Jack.

"You remember everything then?" his father asks.

Jack nods. It's a tight nod, and I can't read what it means. Are things okay between the two of them? How does Jack feel about what Sebastian did? Am I about to get caught between them as they argue?

"I remember," Jack says. "I don't want to talk about it. You should go and prepare for Grayson's Fading."

"Jack-" Sebastian begins.

"I said I don't want to talk about it, Dad. Not now, anyway. Maybe later."

The head of the Underground takes the hint, leaving in the elevator behind us. The moment he leaves, Jack turns his attention to me, and there's an almost frightening urgency in the way he looks.

"When I was unconscious, at the end, you touched me."

"I wanted to wake you up," I say. "Jack, some of the things I saw-"

Jack nods. "I know. I'm sorry you had to see that, Celes."

I shake my head. "I'm not. Your father shouldn't have done that to you."

"I guess he did what he thought was right. With all the people I've faded, I don't know if I get to argue about it. It's not important right now. What is important is that I felt you touch me."

"And?" I'm not sure where this is going.

"And that memory at the end. That one of the woman. I don't think it's one of mine, Celes."

For a moment, all I can do is stand there. "What does that mean?"

Jack bites his lip. It's a nervous habit I haven't seen in him before. "I think it means I'm going to have to do something very stupid now. Come on Celes."

EIGHTEEN

I have to ask. "Jack, what are you planning? I should be going down to see Grayson."

Jack looks slightly pained by that, but he hides it pretty well in the end. "Maybe you shouldn't," he suggests. "It can be harder like that, Celes. Unless you're planning to Fade the memories afterwards?"

I shake my head rapidly. "No. No one takes my memories. Not after all this."

Jack smiles. "At least you probably get a choice in it. After all, it didn't work so well the last time they tried it. I'm sure Dad could have me forgetting all this any time he wanted to."

"Do you want to talk about that yet?" I ask. "I'll listen, if you want."

"I'd like that," Jack says, putting a hand on my arm, "but not now. Now I want to do something that will give you a better idea of who you are. It might even help make things easier with Grayson."

"Easier?" I can't imagine anything making things easier. Grayson is about to forget all about me. "How can you make things easier?"

"By showing you that he isn't what you're destined for, Celes. Your life is about so much more, and I'll show you, if you'll let me."

I can't think how Jack plans to accomplish that. "What are you going to do?"

"Like I said before," Jack says. "I'm going to break the rules. Now, are you willing to go along with me?"

I don't hesitate before nodding. I trust Jack more than enough for this. I have, after all, seen some of the most personal memories he has. He reaches out for my hand, wrapping it in his. It's such a small gesture, yet here and now it feels so very important. Jack leads me to the elevator and presses a button. It's one I don't know, though that could apply to practically all the buttons there, but this one is near the bottom, so I guess that it is important.

When the elevator doors open once more, I know it is.

There's a corridor that looks almost indistinguishable from the one up top, complete with lights that flicker on as we step out into it, except that there are cameras every few feet, and solid looking doors off to each side. Those have retina and palm print scanners outside them, while stern notices warn against attempting unauthorized entry.

Jack leads me over to one of the doors, where he bends to put his eyes level with the scanner for it, while simultaneously pressing his hand against the palm pad. There's an electronic beep, and then the click of a heavy lock unfastening. The door in front of us swings open.

I go to step through it and Jack bars my way with an arm. "Careful, Celes. The security isn't done."

He takes out his gun and places it on the floor outside before stepping into the room. He then holds his arms out wide. Green light plays across his body, and I realize something in there is scanning him.

"Potential recording device detected," a computerized voice says, coming from hidden speakers. "State authorization."

"Jack Alpha Foxtrot Niner," Jack replies. Nothing happens. I assume that's a good thing, because Jack turns towards me. "You can come in now, Celes. When you do, stand still while the security systems scan you. Oh, and you'll need to leave your phone outside."

I do as he says, leaving my phone alongside his gun then stepping inside for the green light to scan me. The computers running the scan don't find anything untoward.

"What's with all the security?" I ask.

"We keep some very important stuff here," Jack replies. "The scans outside are to stop people getting in without someone with the proper clearance."

"And the one inside?" I ask.

"That's to make it harder for someone to force or trick one of us into it," Jack explains. "No weapons are permitted in here, and recording devices or phones need authorization. There's even a safe word that an operative can use to activate the system."

"And when you activate it?"

"The room locks down. No way in or out without the proper codes."

I look around the room. It doesn't seem important enough to warrant that level of security. There are shelves around the walls, each one containing old fashioned box files, but that's it. None of it looks very impressive.

Jack goes over to one of the files. "This is the one we want," he says, taking it out. "I've studied your files, Celes, but I didn't look through everything, and I think there's going to be one thing you're going to want to see."

The file isn't easy to open. There's a thumbprint lock on it, that Jack has to open before we can get in. "So that they know which files we access," he explains.

"So your father will know all about this?" I ask.

"Won't you get into trouble, Jack?"

Jack grins. "I'll just say that you led me astray. Besides, I was in trouble the moment I brought you to this level. We might as well get something out of it." He takes a couple of flash drives out, plugging one into his phone. "My father showed you some of our earliest 'surveillance', right? Only it mostly isn't. Most of it, we take from people's heads. This is some of the very earliest stuff we have for you, Celes."

He turns the phone to me, and I see a woman running with a baby in her arms.

"What we saw in the viewing room," I say.

"Keep watching."

The woman looks fairly normal. She's wearing a long coat and a woolen cap, suggesting that it's cold, but that also means I can't see much of her. She could be anyone, but I can tell that she's scared of something.

There's a dumpster, and the woman goes up to it, placing the baby within. I know this part, because Sebastian played it in the viewing room when I first came in. What I didn't see then is what happens next. The woman runs. She runs, and dark clothed figures run after her. She runs until she comes to a dead end, then she turns at bay like a cornered animal.

She fights furiously, even viciously. She's outnumbered, and several of the men chasing her are armed, yet she still manages to resist for almost a minute, kicking and hitting, throwing men about and hurting them. She fights desperately, as if she knows that the consequences of failing just don't bear thinking about.

Eventually though, she has to lose. There are just too many men for her to fight. One grabs her, and then another, until eventually, they bear her to the ground, finally overpowering her. They pin her quickly and expertly, not giving her a chance to fight anymore. Even then, though, it isn't done. She looks up, and I see her eyes. They're glowing.

It happens in a matter of seconds. She flares so brightly, energy pouring out of her in such amounts that even on Jack's phone, it's hard to look at. It makes even the brightness of burning up the Others back on the road seem like nothing. It burns like a miniature sun for long seconds, and then there's nothing. Nothing at all. No sign of the men in the black outfits, no sign of the woman. Nothing.

I feel my mouth open wide in shock, and I almost fall into Jack. For several seconds, I simply don't know what to say.

"This file is the best record we have of someone doing this," Jack says. "Sebastian...my father didn't want me showing you this, but I think you deserve to know. I don't want to keep secrets from you, Celes."

And he hasn't. In fact, he's broken a lot of rules to make sure that I get to see this. Even so, I need to know more. I can't leave it at just one image, without any kind of explanation to go with it. I can't stand not knowing. There are questions I just have to ask.

"So the baby was me?"

Jack nods.

"And the woman..." I can barely bring myself to say it. "Was she my mother?"

Jack hesitates. Apparently, he hadn't considered that I might say that. "No. Dad... Sebastian thinks she was your nursemaid."

"A nursemaid?" Obviously, these days we have nannies and baby-sitters, au-pairs and all kinds of other people designed to help look after children, but that choice of term seems an odd one. "That seems... I don't know, a bit old fashioned."

"Or just wealthy," Jack points out. "Rich people, important people have nursemaids. And she did a lot to try to protect you. She obviously thought you were important."

Important enough to abandon. Important enough to leave in a dumpster, to be brought up by a family that now doesn't even know that I exist. Sure, she thought that I was important. I know that I'm being petty, though. From the looks of it, this woman gave her life for mine. Certainly, there was no sign of her at the end.

"I don't feel very important," I say to Jack. "I feel like a freak. What she did on this tape, it's what I did to those men back in the field, right? When I killed them."

"Right." Jack says it gently. "From what I can see, it's exactly the same. But that doesn't mean you're a freak, Celes."

"I'm not human, Jack. At least, I assume I'm not. What would you call it?"

Jack shrugs. "You're different, but you aren't a freak. That's part of why I wanted to show you this. To show you that you aren't alone. That there are others like you. Or there were, at least."

"People like the woman on that footage." A woman who was gone at the end of it, probably dead, for all I knew. Yet Jack was right, there was something comforting about knowing that I wasn't unique. A thought comes to me. "Jack, the underground looks for things like me, right?"

"We look into all kinds of unexplained things," Jack says. "I think anyone like you probably counts."

"That really isn't helping on the 'not a freak' front, you know." I look up at Jack expectantly. "How many more like me has the Underground found?"

Jack bites his lip. "Perhaps I shouldn't have gotten your hopes up," he says.

"Jack!"

Jack seems shocked by the force of that, but I have to know. "There are only two instances that we know of before you of someone being able to do what you did to those men," he says. "One is this recording. The other..."

I don't need him to say it, because, thinking back to everything I saw in the viewing room, I already know the answer. "Your mother."

Jack nods. "My mother."

NINETEEN

"And your mother can't explain things, can she?" I say, trying to put it delicately. I saw what happened after all. I saw her die. Saw her vanish.

Jack shakes his head. "No. She can't."

And however bad it is for me, knowing that the last person like me is gone, it must be worse for Jack. After all, with his memories unlocking like that, he now knows what happened to his mother. He knows that she died burning up one of the Others, while he was just in the next room.

"I'm sorry, Jack," I say, reaching out to hold him. It just feels like the right thing to do.

"The worst part," Jack says, "is what my father did. No, it's not even that. It's that I can *understand* what he did."

"What do you mean?" I ask.

"I mean that I've been a part of the Underground so long that if a kid were to come in having seen what I saw, I'd probably want his memories faded too. I'd probably tell myself that it was the best thing for him, the way my father decided it was the best thing for me."

    I hold Jack a little closer. "You'd want it to stop hurting. There's nothing wrong with that."

    Jack shakes his head. "I don't think it does stop it hurting. It just takes away the reason for it, so you're left with this aching hole, and no way to ever make it right. Though my dad has obviously been trying."

    I look at him questioningly.

    "This place," Jack says. "Now that I have the memory, it's easy to see he's been searching for anyone or anything like my mother for years... and now there's you."

    "Yes," I say, holding him closer, "there's me."

    Is that why I feel some sense of connection to Jack? Is it because he's at least partly what I am? Or is it more than that? I need to know, and it seems that Jack feels the same need, because his lips move down to meet mine. It's only a brief kiss, but I don't move back when we're done.

    "So," I ask, "do you get any cool special powers to go with what you are?" I'm trying to keep it light, because it's easier to think about special powers than about signs of being some kind of freak. "Aside from your memories leaking out all over the viewing room, I mean?"

"I guess I'm faster than most people," Jack says. I can practically see him thinking, looking back over his life and trying to pick out which moments might have been more than he thought at the time. "And my reflexes... it's sometimes like I know what's going to happen the instant before it does. Like back at the apartment."

"Like the way you drive," I say.

"What's wrong with the way I drive?" Jack smiles as he says it.

"Do you have... can you..."

He knows what I'm afraid to ask. "I've never been able to put out heat and energy."

It's a much kinder way of saying it than 'burn people alive.' I look up at him. "All this time, and you've had no idea?"

Jack shakes his head. "Da... Sebastian changed me a lot. So much that I'm not sure if there's anything else. I'm just Jack Simple, utterly and completely. He had me trained too. Cars, shooting, fighting. Real fighting, not just martial arts. I used to think that he was just preparing me to be the perfect Fader. Now I'm not sure what to think."

"He wanted to protect you," I guess.

"Yes. And he did everything to manage that except say that there might be a reason why the Others would want to come after me besides my job. I think I hate him right now."

"Don't hate him," I say. "At least we're together thanks to him."

I kiss Jack this time, and it's a much longer deeper kiss. A much better kiss. All the kisses we've had before pale into insignificance beside it. It's not just the passion, though there's plenty of passion. I think it's because we both finally know who the other one is. It's the *real* us kissing this time.

We kiss until I can't think of anything else. We kiss until Jack becomes the whole universe for me. Or maybe we're the whole universe for each other. The last two of our kind, whatever we actually are. For more than a minute, it's enough.

Then an alarm sounds, and we have to come back to the real world. "*Intruders in Sector One!*" an electronic voice blares. "*Unauthorized person free in the facility.*"

I can't help looking around at the door, but it hasn't slammed shut. "Is that for us?"

Jack shakes his head, moving to replace the data drives in their file. "Sector One is the top level. And an unauthorized person..." he doesn't finish that, but runs out, collecting his gun. I pick up my phone and follow, trying to stay close to him.

We head into the elevator, and then up to the viewing room. There are people milling around, all armed. Jack comes in, and they immediately look his way. Apparently, even though he's just one more Fader, he's the closest thing to authority there.

"What's going on?" Jack demands of the nearest Fader, a woman with an automatic rifle.

"A full security breach," she answers. "Multiple personnel coming in on the top level, heavily armed."

Even I know what that must mean. "The Others."

"Exactly," the woman says. The look she gives me isn't friendly.

"What is it, Diana?" Jack demands.

"They've come here looking for her, Jack. They must have. Which means that either they've been able to track her somehow, or that boy she insisted on bringing in told them where to find us."

"Grayson?" I say. "You think Grayson did this?"

"It's the only option that makes sense," Jack replies.

"So they traced him somehow? Homed in on his cell phone or something?"

"Like we wouldn't take that off him?" Diana says. She shuts up when Jack looks at her. But then, with the expression currently on his face, most people would.

"He tipped them off, Celes. This isn't somewhere you find by accident."

I shake my head vehemently. I don't believe it. I *won't* believe it. "Grayson wouldn't do that. He wouldn't betray me."

"Are you sure of that?" Jack demands. "Because it looks like it from here."

I know what it looks like to Jack, but then, he hates Grayson. He has from the moment they met. I know Grayson. He wouldn't do this. He couldn't do this. And I know just what I need to do to prove it to them. I run for the room where they tried to erase my memory and Jack runs after me. He's the only one who can keep up.

I look inside, expecting to see Grayson strapped to the thing. Almost *hoping* to see him there. Yet he isn't, and what I see instead is enough to make me pause at the door, trying to make sense of it all.

There are technicians on the floor, scattered like white coat wearing bowling pins. None of them is moving, and I don't know whether they're unconscious or something worse. Several of them seem to have serious injuries. One's leg is twisted to an unnatural angle, while another is slumped against the wall, a streak of blood higher up showing where he has hit his head. Marlene, the woman who did so much to help transform me, lays a little way from the center of it all, unconscious and very still. It's only when I kneel down beside her that I see she is breathing at all.

Jack stands beside me, surveying the scene. "Well," he says, "that settles it. It looks like Grayson was a plant, Celes."

"No." I say it automatically, standing up to confront Jack. "No, he can't be. He isn't."

"They knew you would go back to visit him if we ever Faded you. They'd get our location without losing track of you. They have been setting up your relationship with him for years for this exact purpose."

"No!"

Jack moves forward, holding me, and it's only when he does that I realize that I'm crying. Grayson... Grayson couldn't do this, could he? If he did, then it means that what Jack said is true. That the Others used him to get here. That they used him to get to me. And that means that I never really knew him at all. All those times we spent together were just to get closer to this point. The times we kissed, or held hands, or just spent time together... none of them are real if Grayson did it all just for this.

"I know, Celes," Jack says, trying to comfort me. "I know it's hard."

"It's... it can't..." What about the attacks on me? Did Grayson have a part to play in them? He wouldn't have set them up, wouldn't have given the orders, because he's too young to be in a position to give orders. Yet he could have told them where to find me. He could have signaled the Others on that day at the running track.

I hear a groan, and Marlene's eyes flicker open. She starts to roll to her side, but makes a sound of pain and stops, clutching her arm.

"Marlene?" Jack says, moving to her side.

"My arm's broken, I think. Oh, it hurts!"

"Lie still," I say. "Don't try to move."

Jack leans over the technician insistently. "Marlene, what happened here? We need to know."

"What happened?" The woman looks up at him. "What happened? The boy happened."

"Grayson," I say.

"We were just getting him ready for the machine. Strapping him in, and he went berserk. He flattened us all, and he ran. He just ran!"

Jack looks across at me. He doesn't say anything. He doesn't need to. The Grayson I knew could never have done this to so many people, but then, it seems that I didn't know Grayson that well at all.

The woman from before, Diana, follows us into the room. She looks around and swears. "The kid did this? I knew he was dangerous. We've got bigger problems than that though. We need to get ready to clear out. Reports from the top levels are that the Others are here in force, sweeping the base room by room."

"Sweeping?" I ask.

"Moving room to room," Jack explains. "Capturing or killing everyone they meet."

"It won't be long until they're down here," Diana says, "so we need to either evacuate or be ready to throw everything we've got at them. And we need to decide now, because the longer we wait, the worse our odds get. What do you want to do, Jack?"

TWENTY

Jack's still trying to make a decision when Sebastian steps into the room. That's almost a shock. When he didn't seem to be around before, I had started to assume that something had happened to him. It makes me wonder what he's been doing in the last few minutes. Coordinating battle plans, probably. Yet he's here now, and he quickly takes charge.

"We're going to stand our ground, Diana," he says, and the Fader who had been talking to Jack before nods an acknowledgement, readying the weapon she carries for use. Apparently, it's the answer she was hoping for. "Now, prepare to evacuate those who can't fight. Everyone in this room is a priority. My jet is waiting at the airfield for them."

Diana the Fader rushes off to start to organize things. Jack remains behind, watching his father. He doesn't seem happy.

"If we're evacuating the injured through the airfield, we have to get them there first," he points out. "Which means going through the Others' lines."

"True. And that won't be easy, when the majority of us will have to stay here to fight."

Jack turns around on his father, obviously upset about that. "So you're prepared to sacrifice everyone here to save this place? Do the people who have devoted their lives to the Underground mean that little to you? I know you Faded me without a second thought, but I guessed you might care about one or two of them."

"We have valuable equipment and information here," Sebastian shoots back, not raising his voice. "Everyone's memories, everyone's records. There's no time to take it with us, so if we lose this place, it falls into the hands of the Others. Then they get our entire network. Hundreds of people, not dozens. Do you want that?"

Jack shakes his head, and I have to agree.

"Do those memories include my parents?" I ask. "My brother's?"

Sebastian nods. "They do."

"Then I'm staying to fight them off," I say, trying to sound determined. I don't know if I succeed. "Those memories are valuable. I'm not going to lose them."

"Celes," Jack says, "you haven't been trained to fight."

"I can still help." I'm determined now. I'm not leaving. One day, my parents are going to get those memories back. They can't do that if the Others have taken them along with everything else in this base.

"I'm inclined to agree with Jack, Ms. Caine."

I shake my head. "I'm doing this."

"Come with me," Sebastian says. "I want to show you something."

He leads the way up to his office above the viewing room, where he activates screens, switching them over from a blur of technical information to what look like security cameras. They show automated defenses slowing down the Others on the top level. There are automated turrets, pinning them down as they try to circumvent them, shock patches on doors that stun individual attackers, and vapor emitters to cut down visibility. Through it all, the Others fight on, hunting down the few members of the Underground still on the top level.

Outside, a small number of cars surround the place. Not enough to constitute a full scale assault, but enough to be a problem. Particularly since there seems to be a much larger group out in the distance, serving as back up, reinforcements, or simply a way of making sure that no one escapes. It's an intimidating sight.

Since they must know that the Underground will have surveillance, it's probably meant to be.

The cameras focus in on a group in one of the upper rooms. They're moving through them with their weapons high, looking for potential targets. Sebastian presses a button, and they all jerk spasmodically, falling to the floor.

"Electrified floor," he explains without being asked. "Jack, take a team up. That should have left a hole for you to punch through and attack the main group outside. With luck, they won't know what hit them."

"Yes," Jack says sounding less confident than usual. Is the situation that bad? He looks at me, his eyes full of concern. "Promise me you'll look after Celes, Dad. I..."

"You love her," Sebastian says, as though it is only to be expected.

Jack nods.

"Very well. Just make sure that you keep focused on what you need to do. We're counting on you, Jack."

I can't believe Sebastian is sending his own son into such a dangerous situation so easily. I step between them.

"Sir, I'm not the one you should be protecting. Jack's injured. He won't be any use out there. Don't send him. Send me."

"Send you to lead an assault?" Sebastian asks.

Jack shakes his head. "No, Celes. It's too dangerous. You're not trained."

"I don't mean to fight them," I say. "But it's obvious they want me. I don't want anyone else here getting hurt because of me."

"I'm not sure that this is just about you," Sebastian says. "And in any case, I agree with Jack. It's too dangerous. You're too valuable. We haven't even begun to understand everything there is to know about you."

I know then that I have to act now if I want to persuade the Underground leader. Otherwise, he'll just pack me off to safety, while leaving Jack to face the Others. Thankfully, it's at that moment that I have an idea.

"We have to hurry, Jack," Sebastian says. "They'll notice the downed team soon enough."

I put a hand on Jack's arm. "Trust me," I say. "I can stop them. And they won't hurt me. Not if they know what's best for them."

That's enough to make Sebastian look at me. "What exactly did you have in mind?"

I swallow. It's now or never. "I'll need a jacket of some kind, along with whatever wiring you can stick to it."

"What are you going to do?" Jack asks. And then he knows, because I feel something pass between us, like a jolt of power. Like whatever happened in the viewing room. As it does, I know that he's seen what I have planned. "Oh no. That's too dangerous, Celes."

"Really?" I ask. "Do you think they want to blow themselves up? You need a distraction, Jack, and this could work."

Sebastian looks from his son to me, and although he obviously isn't happy about it, he nods. "It could," he admits. "And you're brave for suggesting it, Ms. Caine."

"She's not going out there by herself," Jack says. He seems adamant. "Not if I can help it."

"Oh, she won't," Sebastian replies, then looks at me. "I think I have one or two refinements for your plan, dear..."

A few minutes later, I'm on the surface. Jack has gotten me there, he and his team taking out those members of the Others who didn't fall to the electrified floor. I'm wearing a tactical vest wired with enough C4 to blow up a small country. At least, that's what it must look like from the outside. It's actually a patchwork thing put together in a couple of minutes, and which will never explode.

I see the second wave of Others in their vehicles, and I get ready to move over to them. My hand is held high, wrapped around what is actually my cell phone, but which I hope they will assume is some kind of trigger.

"I'll be right behind you," Jack promises, kissing me.

And that's when Grayson rushes over from one of the Jeeps parked next to the base. "No, Celes. Don't."

Jack has his gun up in an instant. So do all the Faders with him. I move between them, but they swarm round me, grabbing Grayson and forcing him to the ground so that they can put some kind of plastic tie around his wrists. He looks up at me with imploring eyes.

"Grayson? What are you still doing here? Did you bring them here? Did you tell them where we were?" I have to ask it.

"No, I swear."

"But you broke out."

"They were going to erase my memory, Celes. Take everything I knew about you. I couldn't... I couldn't forget you. Now, please don't do this."

I know I shouldn't, but I believe him. "I'm sorry," I say. "I have to. It's the best way to stop more people getting hurt. You need to forget me, Grayson."

Grayson shakes his head. "I'll never do that."

In a sudden burst, he's up on his feet, breaking free of the grips of those who hold him. He's stronger than he looks. He's also probably lucky the Faders don't shoot him. "Let me come with you. If you really want to end this without bloodshed, I can help. You can see the Others?"

I look over to where the vehicles are waiting further back. There's a small body of people with them. I nod.

"They're important people, Celes. My father is there. If I take you over, it looks like I've convinced the Underground to give you up. If you need a distraction, that will be a good one. Then Jack can capture them without a fight. The Underground can take their memories."

"You're suddenly willing to do that, when you wouldn't let us Fade you before?" Jack demands in a mocking tone. His gun's still out, I notice. "I don't trust him, Celes."

"Well, what's your plan?" Grayson snaps. "An explosive vest? They aren't going to be that stupid.

They'd shoot Celes before she got close enough to use it. I can get her closer."

I gulp. I hadn't thought of that. After all, the Others tend to be more interested in wiping out threats than talking to them. And they've killed people like me before. I've seen the footage. I look over at Jack. "Can we try it his way?"

Jack starts to protest. "These men are highly dangerous-"

"I'll jump in front of Celes before they can lay a finger on her," Grayson says. "You know I will."

"What I know is that you tipped them off," Jack counters.

"I didn't," Grayson says. "I swear it."

I believe him. I don't think he'd deliberately do something that would put me in this kind of danger. Even though there's so little in my life I can be sure of right now, I'm sure that I would know if Grayson were lying. "I think he's telling the truth, Jack."

"You thought that all the years he was lying to you," Jack points out.

That's enough to make me angry. "I'm doing this," I say, in a tone that doesn't allow for argument. It probably makes me sound like a teenager throwing a tantrum, but I don't care right then. "Now, un-cuff Grayson."

Jack cuts the plastic strip and Grayson gets into the driver's side of the nearest Jeep. I get into the passenger seat.

"Take off the vest," he says. "You'll be safer without it, believe me."

I trust him enough to do it. I also don't like what he said before about the Others shooting me. Grayson looks over at Jack.

"You know I'll keep her safe."

"I know I'll kill you if you don't."

The two stare levelly at one another for several seconds, until I know I have to intervene. "Are we doing this or not?"

Grayson nods. "We're doing this. My father will listen to me. You'll see."

He puts the Jeep in gear and we set off towards the Others' perimeter.

TWENTY-ONE

Gray drives the Jeep out steadily, exactly as we planned. It's a bold move, and I'm relieved to see that the Others appear so surprised at seeing a lone jeep come out of the Underground's complex towards them that they don't fire.

Though that could have something to do with the man at the front of them with his hand up. His temples have Gray hair, and he's dressed like the others, all in black. I recognize him as Grayson's father. Presumably, he's worried that his son would be caught in any crossfire.

We're close now. Close enough that I'm a little nervous. I trust Grayson. Of course I trust him, yet now we're well past the point where the Faders could rescue us if something goes wrong. We're certainly past the point where they can ambush the Others easily. When I mention that to Grayson though, he shakes his head.

"I have to get closer for them to be convinced I have you with me, Celes; that this is peaceful. We can lead them back afterwards."

"Are you sure?" I ask, and fall quiet, because at that point I notice something the Faders should have picked up on. Grayson has a gun in his pocket. It's not enough to frighten me. After all, I don't believe that Grayson would ever use a gun on me, but it's enough to worry me. After all, the Grayson I know wouldn't be carrying a weapon at all.

It's too late at that point, though, because Grayson brings the Jeep to a halt just yards from the Others' vehicles. He steps out, and what I hear him say next makes my blood run cold. "I brought her, just like I said I would." He smiles. "Now let's go get those freaks inside."

My mouth drops open, and a brief wail of anguish comes out. Grayson? *Grayson* could do this? I get out of the Jeep, staring at him. "I... I trusted you."

"And I trusted you!" Grayson snaps back, his eyes flashing with anger. "I loved you once, but you disappeared, and I didn't even know if I would ever see you again. I was a mess, a total mess, and *you* did that."

"I didn't have a choice," I say.

"Yes, you did." Grayson looks at me without compromise. "There's always a choice, Celes, and you chose to hurt me. Well, I chose to stop hurting, and if that means stopping loving you, so be it. You didn't even tell me what you were."

"I didn't know," I insist.

"Liar. My dad knew. When he and his colleagues came to question me, they knew all about you. They *told* me all about you. And from what I've seen, he's right. You're dangerous." He points to the Underground. "They're dangerous for wanting to harbor you."

"I'm not dangerous!" I still can't quite believe Grayson would do this to me.

"Yes, you are." That's from Grayson's father. Richard. I remember his name now. He moves forward, handcuffs in one hand, but Grayson takes them from him.

"I'll handle it," he says, and that only makes it worse, somehow.

I glare at him. At all of them. "You don't even know what I am!"

Grayson's father shakes his head, almost sadly. "I do, Celestra. After all, I'm the one who first caught the news of you, all those years ago."

I try to make sense of that. "But that... that was the Underground."

Grayson's father laughs. "We hadn't quite got to that point by then. You see, I'm a scientist. I explore the unknown. At that point, I was a colleague of someone you might know. Sebastian Cook. We were on the same mission. We worked for NASA, we were among those who picked up the rather interesting signals that come from you. Only they weren't from this planet. They were out close to Mars, and moving rapidly. So you see, Celestra, I do know what you are, and I know where you're from, too."

I don't know whether to be terrified by that or almost grateful. After all, this is one of the few people who can give me the full truth about myself. I've been waiting for this moment almost since the Underground Faded me. I try to look confident.

"What am I then? Where do you think I'm from?"

The older man shrugs. "We have good reason to believe you're the last remaining survivor of a hostile planet close to Mars. Our telescopes and satellites weren't able to detect the planet, but it was always there. By the time we might have detected it though, it was gone."

"Gone?" How can a planet be gone?

"We believe it was destroyed, leaving just a few, very dangerous, survivors behind."

We're back to that theme then. I try to talk to them. I'm not dangerous. I'm just a teenage girl. "If I'm so dangerous, then why let Grayson befriend me, get close to me?"

That doesn't even make Grayson's father hesitate. I know then that he used his son without a second thought. "We didn't know for certain that it was you, at first. After all, the woman and baby we were trying to locate could have been anywhere. Grayson getting close to you gave us the optimum opportunity to observe you."

Observe me. I have to look at Grayson then. "Was that all it was?" I demand. "Was it just you observing me? Doing your father's dirty work? He really put you in danger for that?"

I can barely think of all the things Grayson and I have been through together. We weren't just a couple. We were *friends*. Best friends. We had been for years. And we'd come close to being so much more on several occasions. Only the fact that I had wanted to wait had stopped it.

"You were using me, Grayson."

He looks away, unable to meet my gaze. That's all the answer I need.

"I wish I never met you! That way, I wouldn't have been thinking about you while all this was happening. I wouldn't have come back for you."

"Celes." The force of those words are enough to make Grayson look like he's been slapped. Good. Paler now, he says, "I deserve that. But you have to know... I didn't know anything about this until you left. All that was real. We were real."

His father shakes his head. "Get on with it, Grayson."

Grayson moves towards me, and I decide to add a real slap in the face to the more metaphorical kind. He catches my hand, with reflexes that are far faster than I remember. He's stronger than I remember too as he leans in close to me, looking like he might kiss me.

"Keep this fight going. They're buying it."

What? For a moment I can't make sense of the words. Then it comes to me. This is still part of the act? All of it? I thought... I really thought...

I try to rip my hands clear of Grayson's, but he holds me easily even when I struggle. Then I see it. All the Others nearby are watching. All of them. I'm still too confused to know what's going on, but I know that this distraction is working, real or not. I guide Grayson's hand's down to my waist, and he bends close again.

"Kiss me, and then slap me, Celes. As hard as you can. That will get their attention better than anything."

Gladly. I kiss him quickly, passionately, thoroughly. Then I pull back sharply and hit him as hard as I can. I don't know which feels better in that moment.

"How *dare* you try to get back into my good graces with one kiss!"

"That's not all I want to get back into," Grayson says. That's not something he would ever usually say, but right now I don't know what is normal and what isn't. I don't know what's an act for the sake of the men around us, and what is real. Right now, I'm not sure if I even care.

"After all this?" I say. "You've got no chance."

"Really?" Grayson asks, raising an eyebrow. That gets a laugh from the men around him. Typical. "I think after all this, my chances have gone up. I had to be so careful before, so we never went all the way, but now I know that you're strong enough to handle it, I don't have to hold back anymore."

The men snicker at that. It's embarrassing. It's humiliating. And it's distracting. Oh so distracting.

He kisses *me* then. The first few seconds are firm, almost controlling. Then it's softer as I yield to Grayson's lips, growing to something truly passionate as the seconds go on. His hands are on me, pulling me close, holding me there. I dread to think what it must look like from the outside, or how much some of the Others around us must be enjoying the view. I have to admit though, I'm almost as distracted as they are. Grayson when he's the nice boy next door is one thing. Grayson when he's taking charge, powerful, and only just the right side of scary is quite another.

"What's going on, Grayson?" I whisper, trying to force him to finally make things clear. In spite of my body telling me that it doesn't matter so long as he keeps kissing me, I need to know. I *need* to.

He whispers back, in between kisses. "Celes, don't worry, I'll get us out of this."

So he isn't on the Others' side. At least, I assume he isn't.

"I know you're confused," he says, which is understating things just a little, in my opinion. "*I'm* confused. They memory faded me. They changed so many things..."

"Grayson." His father's voice is firm now. It's the voice of a man who has business to get on with, and can't afford to wait around for his son's amorous adventures to finish. "That's enough. Cuff the girl and get her into one of the cars out of the way. We don't have all day if we're going to finish the Underground."

"...including this," Grayson finishes, spinning away from me and pulling the gun from his pocket, training it levelly on his father's chest. "If anybody moves, he dies."

The Others are still for a moment, apparently trying to decide how seriously to take the threat. At the same time, they don't notice the other threat, in the form of Jack and his team. Jack is racing forward, on the

Others' blind side, with his full team of Faders in tow, sprinting to keep up as Jack moves in on the Others rapidly, his weapon already raised.

That should be a reassuring sight except for two things. The first is that there is almost certain to be a gun battle in the near future with me somewhere near the middle of it. I know that's what I signed on for when I agreed to be the distraction, but that still doesn't mean I have to like the idea of bullets flying past my head.

The second problem is a lot simpler. Jack isn't focused on the Others. I can see, just by looking at him, that his focus is on Grayson. And it looks to me like the only thing on Jack's mind right now is murder.

****

Celes, Jack, and Grayson's stories continues in

Falling (FADE #2)

Releases

October 2011

Kailin Gow

Winner of 2 Awards

EXCERPT FROM

PULSE

By Kailin Gow

****

prologue

She ran like an animal. Her clothes were wet, sopping, clinging to her thighs and to her chest, hollow and transparent around the curve of her shoulders. Her hair shook out droplets of rain; her cheeks were flushed and she was breathless. He could see her heartbeat throbbing at the side of her throat, see it in the rhythmic panting, hear it from across the street, pounding in his ears, intermingled with the thunder bolting from the sky. He could feel it – it felt like an earthquake to him, shaking his ribs, his shoulders, his legs. It had been so long since he had seen a heartbeat like hers – since he had felt a heartbeat at all.

The skies had opened up – as they so often did in North California – without any warning, without any hesitation. It was as if the smooth blue glass ceiling of the world had shattered all at once, letting the primordial oceans pound down upon the pavement. He could see her consternation, her irritation – she wanted nothing but to get out of the rain, to dry herself off, to curl up into
something warm and dry.

But Jaegar loved the rain. He loved the energy – the pulse of life beating down upon the earth. He could hear the scattered raindrops in their rhythmic approach to earth and pretend that each fall of rain was a beat of his dead heart. And she was alive with the energy, too – *alive* as he had never seen a woman alive, tossing her hair back, running into shelter, and her lips were pink and her cheeks were red. He remembered that his lips would never again be pink, that his cheeks would never again be red.

She was so young.

Humans so often surprised him in that way. They looked no different from him – he could have been seventeen; he had been seventeen for so long – but their youth never failed to surprise him. The way the world was so new to them – that rain could still take them by surprise, when he had seen so many rainfalls.

He could smell her. The wind carried her scent to him like an animal's scent, and it was all he could do to keep his fangs in check. He leaned heavily upon the branch and parted the leaves to get a better look at her. He could feel the blood – stagnant in his veins – begin something like a torpid, sluggish, shift towards life – the closest thing he would ever get to a heartbeat. She was the sort of girl who made young boys' hearts pound, he thought – and they never knew how lucky they were to experience that sensation.

For it was the physical aspect of it, he thought, that humans understood least of all. They romanticized vampires, of course – how terrible it would be to live at night! To drink blood! To prey upon humans! These were things they could intellectualize, understand. Humans had been forced to commit murder. Humans had been forced to bite back their most natural, primal desires – and so they could almost understand, when they imagined vampires, what it was like to feel that insatiable hunger for a woman's throat, her breast, her wrist. But not a human in the world had ever been alive without *living*, without a heartbeat – and so they took it for granted – what it meant, that constant linear throbbing, clock-like, towards inevitable death. For Jaegar was a vampire, and he was not alive, and the dull ache in his chest where a heartbeat should have been was for him one of the most agonizing things in the world.

They don't know, he thought. *They'll never understand.*

He had been told that she was the one. He had waited for her until sunset – the sun agonizing upon him, even with the ring around his finger. Vampires were not meant for light, and even the strongest magic could not take away the pain, searing, burning, aching, in his flesh. He was unnatural in sunlight, and only now that dusk was beginning to settle over him could he find relief. He sat perched in the tree, obscured by the leaves, staring at her as she ran down the street.

He leaned in too closely – the birds noticed at last that something was wrong in their midst and took flight; a flurry of wings beat up around him and the branch snapped from the tree and plummeted to the earth below.

It was enough time to make a distraction.

He concentrated, and in half a second he was

behind her, so close he could feel the wind blow her hair upon his lips, and then he opened the umbrella above her.

"Miss," he said.

She startled.

"What the..." She rounded on him.

"You looked wet," he said. She did not seem amused.

"I'm warning you," she said. "I know kung fu."

He had learned kung fu once, many centuries ago. He thought it better not to mention it.

"I'm sorry," he said. "I was just trying to help."

She softened.

"Thanks," she said, lamely. "I'm sorry – I didn't mean to snap at you. But you need to learn not to sneak up on people like that. You scared me."

Her eyes remained fixed upon the tree from which he had come. A suspicious glare clouded her gaze. Had she seen – was she wondering? He knew she knew something was wrong. He tried to maintain whatever pleasant normalcy he could. The sequoias were tall, after all. No human could survive a jump from them – he knew she knew this. He knew she thought he was human.

FADE (FADE SERIES #1)

From Top Author for Young Adults
Kailin Gow

PULSE

17 year-old Kalina didn't know her boyfriend was a vampire until the night he died of a freak accident. She didn't know he came from a long line of vampires until the night she was visited by his half-brothers Jaegar and Stuart Graystone. There were a lot of secrets her boyfriend didn't tell her. Now she must discover them in order to keep alive. But having two half-brothers vampires around had just gotten interesting…

Kailin Gow

EXCERPT FROM

BITTER FROST

****

Prologue

The dream had come again, like the sun after a storm. It was the same dream that had come many times before, battering down the doors of my mind night after night since I was a child. It was the sort of dreams all girls dream, I suppose – a dream of mysterious worlds and hidden doorways, of leaves that breathe and make music when they are rustled in the wind, and rivers that bubble and froth with secrets. *Dreams*, my mother always told me, *represent part of our unconsciousness – the place where we store the true parts of our soul, away from the rest of the world.* My mother was an artist; she always thought this way. If it was true, then my true soul was a denizen of this strange and fantastical world. I often felt, in waking hours, that I was in exile, somehow –

somehow less myself, less *true*, than I had been in my enchanted slumber. The real world was only a dream, only an echo, and in silent moments throughout the day it would hit me: *I am not at home here.*

I would shake the thought off, of course, dismiss it as stupid, try and apply my mother's armchair psychoanalysis to the situation. But then, before bed, the thought would come to me, trickle through the mire of worries (boys, school, whether or not I'd remembered to charge my IPod before getting into bed, whether or not my banner would be torn down yet again from the homeroom message board) – *will I have the dream tonight?* And then, another thought would come to me alongside it. *Will I be going home again.*

And the night before my sixteenth birthday, the dream came again – stronger and more vivid than it had ever come before, as if the gauzy wisp of a curtain between reality and dream-land had at last been torn open, and I looked upon my fantasy with new eyes.

I was a fairy princess. (When waking, I would chide myself for this fantasy – sixteen-year-old girls should want to start a fruitful career in environmental activism, not twirl around in silk dresses). But I was a fairy princess, and I was a child. I dreamed myself into a palace – with spires reaching up into the sun, so that the rays seemed to pour gold down onto the turrets. The floors were marble; vines bursting with flowers were wrapped around all the colonnades. The halls were covered in mirrors – gold-framed glass after gold-framed glass – and in these hundred kaleidoscopic images I could see my reflection refracted a hundred times.

I was a toddler – perhaps four, maybe five years old, decked out in elaborate jewels, swaddled in lavender silk, yards and yards of the fabric – the color of my eyes. I hated the color of my eyes in real life – their pale color seemed to make me alien and strange – but here, they were beautiful. Here, I was beautiful. Here, I was home.

The music grew louder, and I could hear its melody. It was not like human music – no, not even the most beautiful concertos, most elaborate sonatas. This was the music that humans try to make and fail – the language of the stars as they twinkle, the rhythm of the human heart as it beats, the glimmering harmony of all the planets and all the moons and all the secret melodies of nature. It was a music that haunted me always, whenever I woke up.

Beside me there was a boy – a few years older than I was. I knew his name; somehow my heart had whispered it to my brain. *Kian*. All the palace around me was golden – with peach hues and warm, pulsating life – but Kian was pale, pale like snow. His eyes were icy blue, with just a hint of silver flecked around the irises; his hair was so black that ink itself would drown in it. He seemed out of place in the vernal palace that was my home – out of season with the baskets of ripe fruit that hung down from the ceiling, with the sweet, honey-strong smell of the flowers. But he was beautiful, and all the more beautiful for his strangeness.

We were dancing to the music, our bodies echoing the sounds we heard – or perhaps the sounds were echoing us. We were learning the Equinox Dance. It was the dance that we would dance on our wedding day.

It was a custom in this fairy kingdom that royal children would learn this dance – the most complicated and mysterious of all dances – for their wedding days. And so we all practiced, day after day (night after dream-rich night), for the day that we would come of age, and dance the dance truly, our feet moving in smooth unison, echoing the commingling of our souls.

My father was the fairy king of the Summer Kingdom – a place where everything tasted like honey and felt like the morning sun on your forehead. Kian's mother was the Winter Queen of the Winter Kingdom, a place beyond the mountains where cool breezes turned into arctic chill, where a castle made of amethyst stood upon a rocky peak, and evergreens dotted the horizon. And it was only fitting that our two kingdoms should meet, should join together; we were the chosen ones.

"You will be my Queen," the boy whispered to me. His voice was confident, strong.

The dance was still difficult for us. I got tangled in my waves of lavender satin, tripping over his silver shoes. He in turn kept fumbling with his hands, trying to spin me around the waist and instead, elbowing me in the side – but somehow it didn't hurt.

"Silly," cried the other girl watching us. She, like Kian, was stunning – her hair was as long and lustrous as a starless night; her eyes were silver, like the pelt of a wolf. She was called Shasta, I knew. "Silly – that's not how you dance." She giggled, and her eyes glittered with her laugh.

And then everything changed and became chaos – my home was suddenly ripped apart and replaced by a new scene. Something – *something* – was attacking, something with teeth and horns and claws that ripped, something that made a great and bellowing sound I could hear even when I pressed my hands tightly to my ears. *The Minotaur.*

The screaming came from all directions; everybody was running – me and Shasta and Kian – and the adults, all of them – away from the Minotaur, into each other. Everyone had gone mad. And then someone – someone – was fighting it, a cavalcade of fairy knights each shining in his golden armor and some knights from the Winter Kingdom too, in their silver.

The Summer King and Queen were there, and the Winter Queen was there too. She looked like Shasta, but older – and her face was different. There was something hard and glinting in her eyes that I could not see in Shasta's, like the shiny specks in stone. I was afraid.

"This is your fault!" a voice snapped – I could not tell to whom it belonged.

"No – it's yours!" Another voice – equally angry, equally cold.

"If it hadn't been for your kingdom..."

"Don't give me those excuses – the Minotaur is a device of your court!"

The voices grew higher and stranger, angrier, louder, quicker and quicker in their retorts until I felt like I was surrounded in a cacophony of rage, bellowing over and over again until at last all I heard was:

"It's all because of that girl!"

And for a moment, they were all silent, and all of them were staring at me.

I could not understand, but it did not matter. Before I could think, could understand what was going on, what was happening to me, the scene had changed again.

I felt his arms around me. That was the first thing; I felt it before I could see anything, see him. I felt his arms encircle my shoulders, feel him brushing my shoulder blades lightly with his fingertips. I shivered. His hands took mine. I could see him. It was Kian, but he was older, now, and so was I – both a young man and a young woman – staring at each other. Age had only made us more beautiful; his hair was longer, now, and his eyes sharper, with greater depth. I could see my reflection in his eyes; my hair was longer too: a deep, warm brown with flecks of gold studded throughout. And I could see my expression – full of fear, full of joy – as he bent down closer to me, as his lips came ever closer to mine.

"Oh, Breena," he said to me. "My Breena."

His blue eyes took on a look of sharp determination; he stared at me with such intensity that I felt that his eyes had penetrated into the truest part of my true soul, a part hidden even to the rest of this strange and wonderful land.

"I will kill you, Breena. It is what I have to do. It is decreed." He cupped my face with his hands, and I could feel his cool breath whispering upon my cheek. "We are mortal enemies."

Always, every night, that same dream – that same fear, that same joy. When I woke up each morning, I felt a profound sense of loss, a yearning that stretched so deeply it crossed the bounds of reality itself. The alarm clock would ring, and everything would change. I was a nearly-sixteen-year-old girl, with suede boots, with T-shirts bearing sayings I believe in." I had an IPod, a cell phone, my laptop (with pages full of html code for my brainchild, teensforgreatergood.com). I spoke in rushed slang about the latest films and television shows, played video games with Logan, teased him when he won, teased him when he lost. I wore little to no makeup and complained about homework during G-Format. The idea of dating – of fumbling high school boys trying to score in between stolen keg stands, of Facebook relationship statuses and hastily-texted endearments – repulsed me.

Kailin Gow

But for a few hours each night, I was somebody else. I was a princess in a castle, with a dress made of lavender and besides me there is a prince with arctic-blue eyes, and arms wrapped closely around me, and lips coming nightly ever closer to mine...
I was home.

From Top Author for Young Adults
Kailin Gow

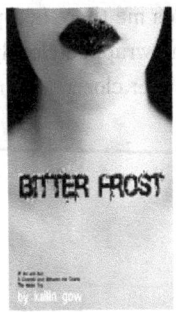

BITTER FROST
All her life, Breena had always dreamed about fairies as though she lived amongst them... beautiful fairies living amongst mortals and living in Feyland. In her dreams, he was always there – the breathtakingly handsome but dangerous Winter Prince, Kian, who is her intended. Then she sees Kian, who seems intent on finding her and carrying her off to Feyland. If she is his intended, why does he seem to hate her and want her dead? And her best friend Logan has suddenly become protective. Things are getting strange...

Kailin Gow

Join the FADE Discussion

Enter

Find out exclusive news, events, previews, teasers, contests and giveaway about

FADE the Series

Join us on Facebook

http://www.facebook.com/pages/Kailin-Gows-FADE-Series/147391975343380